D0899691

The Encyclopedia
of Lies

WITHDRAWN

OTHER BOOKS BY CHRISTOPHER GUDGEON

POETRY
Assdeep in Wonder

FICTION
Greetings from the Vodka Sea
Song of Kosovo

NON-FICTION
An Unfinished Conversation
Out of the World
Consider the Fish
The Naked Truth

HUMOUR
You're Not As Good As You Think You Are

The Encyclopedia of Lies

STORIES

BY

CHRISTOPHER GUDGEON

ANVIL PRESS | VANCOUVER | 2017

Copyright © 2017 by Christopher Gudgeon

All rights reserved. No part of this book may be reproduced by any means without the prior written permission of the publisher, with the exception of brief passages in reviews. Any request for photocopying or other reprographic copying of any part of this book must be directed in writing to ACCESS: The Canadian Copyright Licensing Agency, One Yonge Street, Suite 800, Toronto, Ontario, Canada, M5E 1E5.

Anvil Press Publishers Inc.
P.O. Box 3008, Main Post Office
Vancouver, B.C. V6B 3X5 Canada
www.anvilpress.com

Library and Archives Canada Cataloguing in Publication

   Gudgeon, Chris, 1959-, author

   The encyclopedia of lies / stories by Christopher Gudgeon.

   ISBN 978-1-77214-075-0 (softcover)

      I. Title.

   PS8613.U44E53 2017   C813'.6   C2017-901137-5

Printed and bound in Canada
Cover design by Derek von Essen
Cover illustration by Louis Netter
Interior by HeimatHouse
Represented in Canada by Publishers Group Canada
Distributed by Raincoast Books

The publisher gratefully acknowledges the financial assistance of the Canada Council for the Arts, the Canada Book Fund, and the Province of British Columbia through the B.C. Arts Council and the Book Publishing Tax Credit.

The lamb will sleep another night,
And everything is perfect...

FROM "COUNT FIVE BENZOS"
KEATING GUDGEON, 1996-2016.

Contents

"It's not so much the person, it's the *idea* of Ian I am in love with..."

Elizabeth Wallace nodded and stared at the younger woman, pausing as she lifted her fork to her mouth, the carrot cake impatiently hovering, creating the impression that she, Elizabeth, was indeed listening intently, while all the time she was thinking, *This is exactly the kind of thing that makes Gillian so insufferable.*

"Don't get me wrong, the attraction is still there, there are no problems in *that* department." Gillian Young tilted her head, trying to look demure, letting everyone at the table know that yes, she still had an active sex life — perhaps too active. It was these kinds of teenage antics that drove

The Idea of Ian

the other girls crazy. Still, Elizabeth tried not to show her displeasure. You can't let a person like Gillian get under your skin.

"I love Ian to bits, I really do. It's just, he seems so much more *alive* to me when he isn't there. I must sound the fool."

The other girls assured Gillian that no, she did not sound foolish at all. Analee Frost drew a quick comparison to her stepson's eldest, who was a weatherman (as she never stopped reminding the girls) on a television station broadcasting out of Fort Worth, Texas, a station, again as she never failed to mention, that you could get on the Internet right here in Portland. Analee Frost said she missed her grandson Doug, but felt close to him whenever — and here it comes again — she watched his weather broadcasts from Fort Worth on the Internet.

"That's not what she's talking about at all, Analee." Elizabeth was surprised by the angry tone of her own voice. She softened it a little. "Gillian is not saying that she misses Dean —"

"Ian."

"Hmmm?"

"Ian, dear; you said Dean."

Elizabeth was momentarily confused. Now she'd lost her train of thought, and said so. She took a moment to compose herself. What she was going to say was that Gillian wasn't talking about how she missed her boyfriend (*boyfriend*: what a ridiculous word for people their age!) when he wasn't there, but more how she missed him when he *was* there.

"Distant, is he?"

The girls stopped talking and looked at Elizabeth.

"What's that, dear?" Mrs. Oliver smiled, and Elizabeth could see her grey teeth and a canker of lipstick smudged just above her thin lips. Elizabeth realized that the girls had already moved on from the idea of Ian to another topic.

Elizabeth smiled and *hmmm*ed again. "I was just thinking out loud."

"Well, don't hurt yourself," Gillian said, then repeated herself quickly, looking around the table until all the girls laughed. Even Elizabeth joined in, although it wasn't until much later, at home, that she realized the joke had been at her expense.

It was their regular Wednesday thing; Dutch Lunch, because they went Dutch. The girls had been getting together now once a week for — how long was it? Well, years. Not even Mrs. Roper could tell you for sure. At ninety-seven, Mrs. Roper was the oldest member of the group. She'd been doing Dutch Lunch for almost thirty years. But you ask her and she'd tell you: Dutch Lunch had been going on for years before she got involved.

Elizabeth was standing over the sink — leaning against it, actually — peeling a potato for dinner. Tuesdays were bridge nights with the girls, and she liked to get an early start on supper. It was some of the same ladies from Dutch Lunch but not all of them, and Elizabeth, quite frankly, was thankful for that. Some of the ladies at Dutch Lunch were just a bit too full of themselves.

"Do you want to keep this, Mrs. Wallace?" A boy was standing on her back porch, drops of rain beading his face, holding a wheel from something. It took Elizabeth a moment to recognize him. It was Jackson, the neighbour's son. A teenager. Fifteen, maybe; she couldn't remember. But he looked fifteen. He had the first brush strokes of a moustache. His feet were too big for his body. Jackson was helping Elizabeth clean out the garage and garden shed. She was going to pay him twenty-five dollars, which she knew was probably a lot. But she wanted her garage and garden shed cleaned out and couldn't do it herself. There was just too much junk lying around.

He was holding the tire from a bike, Cissy's bike.

"What is it?" she asked, even though she knew what it was.

"An old tire. I think it's from a ten-speed."

"I guess I should keep it."

"Really?"

"Well, I don't know. Is it useful?"

Jackson shrugged. "I don't know. Not really, I guess."

"Should we put it in the garage sale?" The neighbours were having a big garage sale, seven families, everyone on the cul-de-sac. That's what gave Elizabeth the idea to clean out her garage.

"I don't know if anybody would buy it, Mrs. Wallace. But I guess; you never know."

"Put it in the garage sale pile, thanks Ian."

"Okay, Mrs. Wallace. But I'm Jackson, remember?"

"Hmmm?"

"You called me Ian."

Elizabeth smiled and nodded.

Elizabeth brought a salmon and cream cheese dip to Bridge Night. She had planned to make it fresh, but had fallen asleep after supper. It was the damned weather. Portland just rained and rained this time of year. It wore you out. The weather wore her out and she just had to have a nap. And there you have it. She did not have enough time to make a fresh dip.

"Oh, look," Mrs. Gautier — Larraine — said when Elizabeth showed up. "Elizabeth's here and she's brought her famous salmon dip."

"Good old reliable Elizabeth and her good old reliable salmon dip," someone said. It was probably Gillian Young. That was the kind of thing she'd say.

Elizabeth wanted to say, *What does that mean, "good old*

reliable Elizabeth and her good old reliable salmon dip"? But she held her tongue. She wasn't going to let someone like Gillian spoil Bridge Night. Instead she just smiled and looked for a place to sit down.

Mrs. Lu, the Chinese widow, was not there that night. She had just had her gall bladder out and was still recovering. She was a good card player and very quiet. She was Elizabeth's regular partner, and somehow Elizabeth got stuck with Gillian Young as her partner. Gillian was not a good partner. She talked all the time and could not keep track of her cards. And she had no idea how to bid. She would pass when she shouldn't pass, or open when she shouldn't open. Elizabeth had tried I-don't-know-how-many times to teach Gillian how to count her cards properly, but the woman just couldn't get it. They didn't win a single rubber.

At nine o'clock, they took a break for dessert and Analee Frost made everybody watch the weather report from Fort Worth, Texas, on the computer. Elizabeth sat by herself at the kitchen table and finished off two pieces of Larraine Gautier's Lemon Slice and pretended to flip through a gardening magazine. She was feeling angry about how she had got saddled with that stupid woman as her partner, and decided to sit by herself and bite her tongue rather than run the risk of saying something rude.

After dessert, they started playing another rubber. Elizabeth and Gillian were partnered against Mrs. Lazlo (who, like Elizabeth, had recently lost her husband) and Larraine Gautier. Gillian opened the bidding with two hearts. Elizabeth came back to her with two spades, but when it came back around to Gillian, the stupid woman switched to diamonds — diamonds! It made no sense at all. Elizabeth found herself the dummy hand, and had to sit there like a mouse watching Gillian Young lose trick after trick, all the time chattering like a bird about nothing.

"It's no wonder he left you." Elizabeth heard herself speaking. She knew she was angry but could not help herself.

"Who left who, dear?" It was Mrs. Lazlo, whose husband, Neal, had been an ophthalmologist and done very well for himself. The ladies had stopped playing their cards and were all smiling at Elizabeth now.

"Your *boyfriend*, Gillian. It's all the incessant nattering. Men don't like that."

The ladies were still smiling. Gillian Young tilted her head like a curious canary. "Ian? Are you talking about Ian, dear?"

Elizabeth pushed herself to her feet, banging her shin in the process, and walked toward the front hallway. She could feel her heart racing and had intended to leave right then and there, but caught herself at the last second. She turned and excused herself, as calmly as she could muster, and went off to the bathroom. She stood by the vanity, her hands on the counter, for several minutes, breathing slowly, until the anger subsided.

When she returned to the living room, she apologized and said that she was feeling rather under the weather all of a sudden and had to leave. The girls all made a fuss, and Mrs. Lazlo wanted to call her son Ted, who lived nearby, to drive Elizabeth home. She thanked them all, but turned down the offer of a ride.

She was tired when she got home from Bridge Night, tired and angry. She was upset that she had let a woman like Gillian ruin the evening for her. She looked forward to Bridge Night all week. She could feel her heart racing again, and was a little out of breath by the time she sat down in the recliner beside the big chair — "Des' Chair" — and picked up the channel changer. She began slowly clicking through the channels. She liked to watch detective shows in the evening and liked British detective shows best. The actors were very good and there was not too much violence. The characters were ordinary and funny, just like she liked them, and the stories weren't too complicated. If there was a mystery — and there always was — Elizabeth liked to be able to figure it out before everything was revealed at the end.

She turned on PBS and there was a British detective show on, although she wasn't sure which one. She thought of making herself a cup of tea — she always felt like making tea when she watched British detective shows on PBS — but didn't want to get up again. She took a deep breath and put her feet up on the ottoman. One show, then to bed. She adjusted the cushion so her back didn't hurt so much. She turned the volume up, and then, instinctively, reached her hand toward the big chair, holding it there for several seconds. When she realized what she was doing, she pulled her hand back and let it fall to her side, then slid the small recliner further back until she was almost lying down. She turned the volume up even more and closed her eyes, her head filled with the sound of those wonderful British actors with their wonderful British accents until, finally, she fell asleep.

There were two of them, black guys. I don't know why that surprised me, but it did. I guess I thought one cop would be white, one would be black, for diversity or something.

"You his boyfriend?" the one cop, the shorter guy, asked as his partner lifted his leg to kick the bedroom door open.

I shook my head.

"We just hang out a lot."

The short cop nodded and looked up at me with those sad, watery eyes that black guys sometimes have, and I felt for a second like I wanted to hug him. It's stupid. You don't randomly hug people and you especially don't randomly hug a cop. But I felt like I wanted to hug him or, rather, I felt that I wanted him to hug me.

Jericho

"Valentina and the Arab were in Orlando," I said.

We were driving the 405 just outside Lakewood, in a rented Camaro convertible — white-girl white — listening to old-fashioned Mexican music on the radio because that was the kind of music Jericho liked to listen to when he got high.

I wasn't sure Jericho heard me overtop the moaning mariachi trumpet, so I said it again.

"Everybody was in Orlando," he said, after a bit.

Jericho was hanging his head out the window even though the top was down. He was taking in all the air he possibly could.

"*Te ver como pinche perro,*" I said.

"Your Spanish is shit."

Jericho was wearing a blue tank top and a denim

17 •

jacket, even though the sun was high and it was hot as fuck. He took a joint out of his pocket, still singing now and then, and tried to lick it. But he kept missing his mouth, unable to steady himself as I cut from one lane to the other, and unable to steady his unsteady hands because of whatever it was that made them shake all the time.

"I fucked him once."

"You fucked who, Jer? Valentina?"

Jericho didn't answer, he just sat there with his long hair — dyed an even whiter white-girl white — flying all over the place, every once in a while opening his lips just enough to sing along with the sad-sounding Mexican singer and his sad-sounding song.

"Likes it kinda rough," Jericho said, after a time.

"Valentina?"

Jericho repeated what I said — "Valentina" — and giggled, reminding me how young he was. He acted so serious all the time that you'd think he was already in his thirties. But when he laughed, his eyes drooped and he got this stupid look on his face, scrunching everything up as if even laughing hurt, and you remembered: he was almost still a kid.

Jericho finally got the joint in his mouth and was patting his pockets, trying to find a lighter. He opened the glovebox, all the time singing in that hard Mexicano.

"Why do you listen to that shit, Jer?"

"It reminds me of my childhood."

"You had a childhood?"

Jericho giggled again, then leaned back, shut his eyes and held one shaking hand up, opening and closing it like he was trying to grab the air, singing along now to a new song that had come on the radio, an even sadder song sung by what sounded like two ladies, almost in sync but not quite.

"What are they singing about? Love or something, right?"

Jericho looked at me, never answering, just singing and singing and pushing his white, white hair out of his eyes with those hands that shook and shook no matter what he did with them.

First time I met Jericho he was living at Victor's place and working as a shot boy at a club on Santa Monica Boulevard. I'd just got fired from the call centre and had gone into the bar to drown what little sorrow I had left. And there he was, walking around shirtless, selling Jell-O shooters from a tray. Slim, short, his eyes are big; he isn't perfect.

I bought two shooters and gave him a twenty-dollar tip.

He told me his name was Enrique but everyone called him Jericho. He'd just moved to L.A. from Austin. I'd never met a guy from Austin but I loved the way the name sounded, so the fact that he was from there and exactly my type seemed exotic and perfect.

Jericho told me that his mother had thrown him out. She was a Jehovah's Witness or something and she'd kicked him out after she found him in bed with his boyfriend. He'd come to L.A. because he had nowhere else to go.

"There's like forty-nine whole other states," I said.

Jericho shook his head and said something in Spanish.

"I bet your boyfriend was fucking cute," I said.

"My boyfriend," Jericho said, a big smile on his face, "was a total fucking asshole."

We'd done some lines in the staff restroom, then made out for a bit. Nothing hardcore, just kissing and feeling each other up. I was sitting on the toilet and Jericho was straddling my lap. I'd slipped my hand down the back of his pants and squeezed his perfect little ass and told him how beautiful he was. Jericho'd tried to smile, but whatever he did to his face just made him look a little scared.

Maybe he was preoccupied. I suppose he could have got fired or something if anyone caught us. But in time I came to realize: he was just one of those guys who, deep down, thinks they're ugly even though everyone else thinks otherwise — the world is full of guys like that — and maybe me paying him a compliment about his looks only reminded him of how far removed he was from his own beauty.

We'd done a couple more lines and made out some more and at one point Jericho'd pulled my dick out of my pants, then took one look at it and started laughing.

"I was gonna suck you off, man, but I don't think I could fit that thing in my mouth."

"You give up too easy," I said.

"Giving up easy is what I do best," Jericho'd said, and then he laughed again, a sad laugh that almost wasn't even a laugh at all. Just a kind of unhappy groan that made me like him even more.

"Why don't they have lighters in cars anymore?"

Jericho asked the question very seriously, like he was asking a bigger question about the relationship between happiness and suffering or the contrary nature of beauty, which brings one great pleasure while inflicting a certain kind of pain.

I shrugged.

"Something to do with political correctness or something, I guess."

We were listening to a single trumpet play a sharp, wandering melody. I called it bullfighter music and Jericho smiled, repeating the phrase to himself, kind of distracted, like he was listening to me but not really paying attention.

Victor's place had been just around the corner and I said something about it to Jericho. He was watching a homeless man — his dirty stuff piled high in a Walmart cart — cross the crosswalk.

"Victor had a stroke or something, right?"

Jericho didn't answer. I didn't really expect him to, but I wanted to ask the question anyway.

"Have you ever noticed," Jericho said, as the homeless guy struggled to push his cart up onto the curb, "that no matter how many people you know, how many friends you have, how much money you spend, how many things you own, you are basically always completely alone?"

"I think you're fucking high," I replied.

Jericho giggled his little gay-boy giggle, then pulled a fresh pack of Winstons from his shirt pocket. He tried to unwrap them, but his hands were shaking so bad — he gave up and threw the pack on the seat between us.

We were on our way to see Valentina, a Brazilian drag queen who lived in Bel Air with his boyfriend, who was a bit of a nutjob. Jericho owed Valentina nine hundred and fifty dollars. I don't know why; I tried to keep myself out of that side of Jericho's life. I just know that he was always owing someone something.

Jericho took his phone out of his pocket and held it up. He tried to type something with his shaking hands.

"If I had a motto," he said, all very serious again, "I know what it would be."

"Why would you have a motto, Jer?"

"That's not the point."

He put the phone down on his lap, then patted his pockets, this time for I don't know what.

"The point is," he said, "if I did have a motto, I know what it would be."

He put his head back, like he was going to try and sleep, but then he just started giggling like crazy.

I looked at him as if to say, *What's so fucking funny?* But he just kept giggling and giggling until he couldn't even catch his breath. Finally, he took a couple deep breaths and got a hold of himself.

"Well?" I asked.

"I was just thinking about what you said."

"I said a lot of things."

Jericho didn't respond. He just sat there, smiling, singing to himself, every once in a while giggling again to whatever it was that was making him giggle.

Do you want a coffee or something?" the shorter cop asked. His partner was already in Jericho's room.

"To be perfectly honest," I said, "I would love a glass of water."

His name, he told me, was Darnell, which struck me as funny because it was such a perfect black guy name. Darnell'd been with the LAPD for seventeen years.

"I've never been with anything for seventeen days let alone seventeen years," I said.

I smiled at the short cop and he looked at me with his watery black-guy eyes, then offered me a cigarette.

"Jericho doesn't like people to smoke in the apartment."

"I think he'd make an exception in this case."

I took the smoke and leaned forward for a light.

"What did it mean?" Darnell asked as I took my first drag.

"What did what mean?"

"The thing he wrote. The thing in the note."

Jericho had left a note taped to his bedroom door. It was folded in half and on the front he'd drawn a little heart with an arrow running through it. Inside he'd printed a single sentence: *Look into the eyes of the Dragon,* — he'd wrote — *and despair...*

"It was like his motto," I said, "or would have been his motto if he had one."

Darnell nodded as if the relatively incomplete and incongruous thing I had just said made perfect sense to him.

"It's from a poem or something, right?" he asked.

"It's from a movie he liked, from when he was a kid."

"I never read poems. They do nothing for me."

I repeated what I said, about it being a line from a movie Jericho liked, but Darnell didn't seem to hear me.

He just stared at his hands for a second, then stubbed his cigarette out on the chipped saucer we were using as an ashtray.

He stood up. "You okay?" he asked in a way that made you feel he wasn't just asking, he wasn't just doing his job, but that he actually wanted to know.

I shrugged and nodded and looked at him and those wet eyes.

"How long were you . . . were you guys friends?" Darnell asked.

"A long time," I said. "Sixteen, maybe seventeen days."

Darnell smiled and put his hand on my shoulder and squeezed just a bit. Then he smiled again before wandering off toward Jericho's bedroom.

We stopped at The Bayou in West Hollywood and ordered a couple Jägerbombs. We were already running late, but that didn't matter. Jericho was still like four hundred dollars short and in no hurry to get anywhere. Besides, everyone knew that Jericho was always late for everything.

The place was almost empty except for the bartender and this old guy sitting by himself at a table in the corner. I'd seen the old guy around now and then, always sitting by himself, drinking rum and Cokes or something like that. He barely ever talked to anyone, just sat at the same table, by himself, very quiet and still except for every once in a while, when he'd pull out a comb and run it through the near-extinct hair on his impossibly big head, an almost perfect egg-shaped thing with this tiny, unhappy face pinched into the very middle.

The bartender was drinking a coffee and watching the

news from Orlando with the sound off: a chunky reporter standing in the middle of the street in front of the
nightclub, which was still wrapped in yellow tape. The
reporter was talking to a couple gay guys. You couldn't
hear what they were saying, but the one gay guy was crying and the reporter was crying too.

"I went to Orlando once," the bartender said, to nobody really. His voice was shaking a little and you could
tell he was still upset. "We almost went to that club, but
there was a lineup to get in so we went somewhere else."

"I went to Disney World in Orlando with my aunt
when I was a kid," Jericho said. "It's way better than Dis-
neyland, if you ask me."

And then the four of us — me, Jericho, the bartender
and the old guy — went quiet. I looked back at the TV. A
different reporter was talking to a lady now, a mother or
maybe a sister or something. The lady was sitting on a
couch in what I supposed was her living room, while the
reporter, a Latino guy, sat in a chair across from her. The
lady was crying and crying, lost in her specific grief,
while the reporter sat there, holding his clipboard on his
knee, looking grim in that fake grim way reporters have.

The lady was crying and crying and trying, I think, to
say something, and the reporter was sitting and sitting
and trying to look grim, until a funny thing happened.
It just came and went, in a second maybe, but it was
there all the same, a look of real pain that flashed across
his face. You could see it in his eyes and at the edges of
his lips, like he was straining not to cry, straining to
retain his composure, straining to remain a reporter in
the face of all this unhappiness and sorrow. And for a
moment, you could see his hand move toward the

woman, an almost imperceptible motion, and I think he wanted to reach over and touch her and maybe hold her hand and say some words of comfort. But he stopped himself, pulled his clipboard close to his chest and made himself look all grim again.

"Can I buy you and your boyfriend a drink?"

The old guy with the big head was talking to Jericho from across the room.

Jericho checked the guy out for a minute, taking in his big egg head and his unhappy little face.

"He's not my boyfriend," Jericho said, after a bit.

"Can I buy *you* a drink then?"

Jericho shrugged. "You can sure try."

The old guy sent a couple Jägerbombs over, and Jericho downed his in a single shot. A second later he was up and walking over to the old guy's table.

I can't tell you what Jericho and the old guy talked about but I'm sure Jericho was trying to get some money out of him. Maybe he was giving the old guy a sob story — Jericho had a lot of them and, frankly, most of them were true — or offering to suck him off or whatever. I tried to keep myself out of that side of Jericho's life. I just know that he had a way of getting money out of people in general and old guys in particular.

I drank a couple beer and smoked the last of Jericho's Winstons while I waited for him to come back. I don't know exactly where they'd gone — I assumed back to the old guy's place. That was the nature of our relationship. Jericho was always leaving me somewhere while he went off with someone.

And then he was back again, his hair wet, smelling of some kind of flowery old-guy shampoo. I could tell he was a little high on something. Coke maybe? Meth?

Jericho pulled a roll of bills out of his pocket, paid our bar tab in cash. He dropped a fifty-dollar bill in the bartender's tip jar.

The bartender looked at him with a happy, what-the-fuck face.

"In honour of Orlando," Jericho said, which only just confused the bartender more.

Valentina answered the door in his housecoat. It was short, barely reaching his nuts, and was covered in red flowers that weren't roses but almost looked like roses. He was holding a bottle of eyeliner in one hand; he must have been doing his makeup when we knocked.

Valentina was maybe thirty-five or forty and beautiful even with his makeup half-done.

He invited us in but Jericho said we couldn't stay. Valentina looked genuinely upset.

"I've got a little meth," he said, "if you want to get high."

Jericho shrugged.

"Sorry, baby," he said, as he handed Valentina a wad of bills.

I watched Valentina count the money. He was very meticulous, rearranging the bills as he counted so they all faced the same way.

I'd seen Valentina perform in drag a few times. He

was good. He danced with a bunch of plastic fruit on his head, a kind of Latin dance where he'd move his feet and hips real fast, shuffling backwards and forwards in time to the music. Everybody loved it, even the "straight" guys — the Latino daddies and closet cases who'd come to the club just to watch Valentina whenever he performed.

"There's only like four hundred and seventy dollars here," Valentina said, after counting the money a second time.

"Sorry, baby. That's all I got."

"Argo's not going to be happy."

"You can tell Argo," Jericho said, as he leaned forward to kiss Valentina goodbye, "to go fuck himself."

The first thing I did was call 911. The lady on the other end asked me if I wanted police, fire or ambulance.

"Police, I guess. Probably should send an ambulance too, I guess."

The lady didn't get flustered. She asked me to explain the situation.

"I don't know what the situation is," I said, and then I told her about the note and how I'd tried to open the door, but it was locked.

I was waiting for her to get mad at me for not kicking the door down or whatever. But she didn't get mad at all. She just told me she was dispatching the police, and then asked me if I was okay.

"I'm good, yeah, I think. Should I do something?"

"You sit tight, son—" those were her exact words. "The police will be there in a couple minutes. You just sit tight and let them take care of everything."

I tried to keep my mind occupied, but I kept going back to the note and the fact that Jericho was in the room beside me in whatever condition he was in. I wished I was one of those guys who could do something in a situation like this, like administer CPR or something, and I wished I could have done something to help him before it got to this. I don't know what I could have done, though. All I could have really done is talk to him and I did that all the time.

I shut my eyes and placed my hands on my knees. I thought I should cry or something, that that would be the appropriate thing to do. But I didn't. I just sat there, hands on my knees, cigarette still pinched between my lips, breathing in smoke and distant conversation, wishing someone would come and turn off the light so I could be alone in the darkness.

We never actually fucked, me and Jericho. We came close one time, when he was still living in the room above Victor's garage. But that was it.

Fact is, there wasn't a lot of chemistry between us. Maybe there was at the beginning, but it was mostly me. He was my type — beautiful, sad — and while you couldn't really say that he had a type, you could say that there was a particular thing he was looking for at that particular time. I'm not sure if he knew exactly what it was, I just knew it wasn't me.

Anyways: it was probably like the third time we'd hung out and I'd gone over to visit Jericho in that room above Victor's garage, tiny — barely big enough for Jericho's La-Z-Boy and a dresser. We'd smoked four or five bowls and got so fucking high that we went into Victor's room and jumped on the bed for like an hour, laughing until we couldn't breathe anymore, and then we'd turned on each other all of a sudden, without saying anything, and stripped each other naked right there on Victor's bed, for no reason other than we wanted to be naked at that particular moment in our lives.

And even as I was pulling his pants off one leg at a time, feeling his fingers holding my hair tight, tugging it, hurting me just a little, I could see the sadness in his eyes.

"I never fuck on a first date," he said, slipping one hand around my throat.

"This is like our third date."

Jericho didn't say anything. He just tightened his grip a little, lay his head on my chest and played with himself. And even though I wanted to fuck him, or rather, wanted him to fuck me, I just put my arm around his shoulder and softly rubbed his back till I felt his body tighten and felt him come all over my stomach.

And then we just lay there for I-don't-know-how-long, me rubbing Jericho's back, 'til he fell asleep with his head on my chest, and I kept rubbing 'til I fell asleep listening to the sound of him almost, but not quite, snoring.

We were driving, Darnell and me, back from the rental place in Lakewood. He'd followed me in the cop car and worked it out with the Avis guys so I didn't have to pay the late fee on the Camaro.

We'd been quiet for a while, as we drove the empty streets to the sound of some weird country music on Darnell's iPhone.

"Aren't you supposed to listen to the police radio or something?" I asked eventually.

Darnell looked at me and smiled, not answering my question, just mouthing the words of the country song like, if he'd been actually singing, he'd have been singing his head off.

It had taken them four or five hours to finish up in Jericho's room. There were all kinds of people in the apartment by then. More cops had arrived shortly after Darnell's partner kicked the door in. And then not one but two sets of ambulance attendants showed up. Finally, a truck full of firefighters arrived, six or seven of them, in their black and yellow coats and rubber boots. Everyone seemed to know everyone else, which, for some reason, made me feel a little better.

I had to go through the story like ten times. We'd stopped at a bar on Santa Monica, I'd told them, on the way back from Valentina's. Jericho had been quiet most of the way. I didn't know if it was because he was thinking about the Arab and what he might do or if it was just because we'd smoked up when we'd got back to the car and Jericho was one those guys who got quiet and introspective when he got high.

We'd stayed at the bar maybe an hour and a half, and Jericho'd had two, maybe three beer, so I can't say he was really drunk. He sure didn't act drunk on the way home and he sure wasn't acting depressed or anything like. No more depressed than usual, I suppose.

I'd taken him home and dropped him off while I'd gone up the street for Chinese food. Jericho'd seemed fine when I left him; he was just hungry and wanted Chinese food, and once he'd suggested it, I'd wanted it too.

I was gone only like half an hour. When I came back, I could hear sad Mexican music coming from his room and saw the note taped to his door. My first thought was he'd run away and he'd left a note to tell me. It was a stupid thing to think but that's what went through my head, that Jericho'd run away and left a note to say goodbye.

I looked at Darnell again. He was focused on driving, still mouthing the words to the country song, but less intensely now as he carefully looked around, on the lookout, I supposed, for bank robbers and drug dealers and kidnappers and murderers.

Watching Darnell sing and not sing made me happy and sad at the same time, and for the second time that night I thought I should cry. I even tried to make some tears form in my eyes. I thought about the saddest things I could think of, then realized that the saddest things I could think of were no sadder than the everyday normal things I experienced all the time.

And as I sat there, trying but unable to cry, watching Darnell move his lips in sync to the country song as he scanned the streets with his sad, wet eyes, I felt once again like I wanted to hug him or, rather, like I wanted him to hug me. For a moment I imagined sliding my hand toward him until my fingers touched the very edge of his pant leg, just above the knee.

And I actually started inching my hand across the car seat until I thought better.

You don't randomly touch the legs of people and you especially don't randomly hug a cop or randomly rest your fingers up against the leg of some cop you just met.

And just because you feel an attraction for someone —
or just because someone is nice to you for no good reason
other than they are just being nice — it doesn't mean they
like you any more than they like any other random person
they just met. Maybe it's just so rare that people are nice
to us for no good reason that we forget that that's how
people are actually supposed to be.

As I sat there, all this stuff running through my head,
Darnell looked at me with his wet, sad eyes and asked me
one more time if I was okay.

I nodded again, shut my eyes, laid my head back.

"You're probably in shock," he said. "It might be days
— weeks: and then it'll hit you, all at once."

I didn't say anything, I just tried to shut out the sound
of the country music and think only about my next cigarette and how good it was going to taste and how I could
hardly wait to get back to my place and get myself alone
and open the window and light that cigarette up and
breathe in the cool night air between long drags and look
up at the stars.

That's what I most liked to do when this kind of stuff
happened, hard stuff, like losing Jericho. At times like
this, I most liked to be alone, find a place, dark and
quiet, to smoke and look at the stars and try not to think
about things, try not to let my mind wander, try not to
think about pain and heartache and the sad things that
happen to us all, try not to think about all the people
who come and go in our lives, try not to consider the
deeper questions, like, what is the point of love when,
at the end of the day, it only leaves you sadder and more
alone than when you started, or how come, despite all
your best efforts, everything good always ends with a

locked door that you can never — even if you really want to — open.

One day, Diane decided to win that fifty thousand dollars. She took the afternoon off from the call centre, borrowed Lenny's brother's video camera, and took Bird and Mose to High Park.

"Do something funny," she said.

Mose looked around, then dropped to his butt. Bird did a silly dance, which was funny in a way, but not in the kind of way that would win Diane the fifty thousand dollars.

"Try running up there a bit," Diane waved them up the muddy hill.

She thought that maybe they might slip and fall down. Maybe they'd even slide a bit in the mud. That would be funny.

Life before Video

But Bird scooted up the hill without a problem, and Mose, when he finally got off his butt, walked about halfway up before his boot fell off. He couldn't get it back on, and started to cry.

Diane was running out of good ideas, when she spotted the old crabapple tree on the far side of the park, past the swing sets.

"Last one to the tree's a rotten egg!" She learned to make everything a game. That way you didn't have to yell so much. That way, it was a lot easier to make it through the day.

Bird took off like a shot and even Mose stopped crying and joined in the fun. He picked up his boot and ran in that funny Frankenstein way two-year-olds have. Diane took a picture of that, not because she thought it'd win the fifty thousand dollars, but because she liked it. Mose looked cute when he ran. Maybe, when he was a teenager, she'd show the picture to Mose's girlfriends, so they'd know what a cute little kid he'd been.

By the time Diane reached the crabapple tree, Bird was halfway up. Mose stood at the bottom, his hand on the lowest branch, waiting for a boost.

"Look Mommy. I'm a monkey. Ee-eee! Ee-eee!"

"That's right Birdy-bird, be a monkey. Let's see you swing."

Bird didn't get one swing in when the branch broke and he fell right on top of Mose, knocking Mose's head into the trunk of the tree.

He didn't cry right away. Those were the worst ones, when he didn't cry right away. When he took a second to lead up to it, then let go with a real cry, when his face got all red, those were the worst.

Bird was lying there too, on his back, crying, but no blood or anything, just the wind knocked out of him.

Diane wiped the blood away from Mose's mouth and saw that it was just a cut on his lip. Thank goodness Mose hadn't lost a tooth; the last thing Diane needed right now was a dentist bill. And even though he was crying, he managed to smile when she asked him to smile for Mommy, a little sad brave smile through the tears, and she could see that his teeth were fine.

Diane picked up Mose and Bird, both of them still crying, and walked a few yards to the video camera. She put down Bird, picked up the camera and shut it off, picked up Bird again and walked back toward the bus stop.

On the way, Diane slipped on the muddy hill. She slid right to the bottom of the hill. It didn't seem funny. It only pissed her off some more.

Jackson was reading a book on ancient Egypt, *Inside the Ancient Pyramids*. Not made-up stories, but real history.

Jackson did not like made-up stories, and that is mostly why he hated English at school. English at school was about poetry and Shakespeare comedies that weren't funny and short stories that had sudden, remarkable twists at the end. These were the kinds of things that bored Jackson and, frankly, he didn't like the way the writers of those kinds of books tried to trick you. Life did not have twists; sure, sometimes things happened that you didn't expect. But these things were never remarkable, and when observed from the proper perspective — a historical perspective — they made perfect sense.

The Milwaukie Book of the Dead

His friend Erik had given him a different book called *Alien Landscapes: Solving the Mystery of the Great Pyramids!* It was written by a Russian scientist named Vladimir Solonnikov who claimed that the gods of ancient Egypt were in fact extraterrestrial visitors — aliens who had built the pyramids and mated with humans, becoming progenitors of the line of pharaohs. There was even DNA evidence found in tissue samples taken from Tutankhamun's mummified remains, the author said, strains of genetic material that were found nowhere else on Earth. In fact, Solonnikov claimed, the entire concept of mummification was something the Egyptians had learned from the aliens, who themselves took great care to preserve the bodies of their dead so they could bring them back to their home planet for proper burial. Solonnikov went on to write that other wonders of the ancient world — the mysterious ruins of Puma Punku, the giant stone sculptures of Easter Island, the geoglyphs of Nazca Desert, etc. — were also remnants of alien contact. *Why is the government hiding the truth from us?* The words were printed in a bright red font on the cover of *Alien Landscapes*, letters so bright and so red that it almost hurt Jackson's eyes to look at them.

Jackson did not believe that the pyramids — or anything else — had been built by aliens. It seemed stupid to think that an advanced race of time-space travellers would journey all the way to some obscure planet in a distant galaxy just to construct a giant stone edifice and trick a bunch of ignorant people into worshipping them. He preferred the truth: the pyramids were constructed by teams of engineers, working with hundreds if not thousands of master craftsmen, who toiled long and hard to produce something very human that strove to reach to the feet of God and beyond, directly connecting the world of ancient Egypt with the eternal mysteries of the universe.

"The Egyptian pyramids originally had jagged edges like Mayan pyramids, but they were worn down by a thousand years of sandstorms," Jackson was reading out loud to Erik, who sat at the opposite end of the dining room table. Jackson had *Inside the Ancient Pyramids* open in front of him. Erik, who was a really good artist and could probably someday go on to work for an animation company or game designer or something like that, was drawing a picture of the Zombie Apocalypse: a beautiful lady, her sheer dress clinging to her body, brandishing a sawed-off shotgun as a horde of undead marched relentlessly toward her.

"Solonnikov believes the Mayan pyramids were also built by aliens and, in fact, predate the Egyptian pyramids by several thousand years." Erik stayed focused on his drawing as he spoke. He was working to get the nipples — their erect outline was visible through the dress — just right.

"That's not true. Egyptian civilization is like two thousand years older than Mayan."

"That's what the scientists *want* you to believe."

"Why would scientists care what I believe, other than if it's the truth?"

"Because knowledge is power, and they are all part of the conspiracy to keep the truth about the real origins of civilization hidden from us."

"That's stupid. You don't even believe that."

"I don't know. Maybe I do. Parts of it, anyways."

The two boys sat for a moment, silently enjoying one another's proximity, although maybe not each other's company. Erik had been coming over to Jackson's house a lot lately, and sometimes Jackson just needed a break. He definitely liked Erik — they were friends and everything — but it's hard to pretend to be nice to someone all the time. He felt kind of obligated to be nice to Erik, since Erik's parents had split and he and his mom had had to move into the 'burbs. And it was like his dad said: Erik missed having a mother and father at home, and a home without a mother and father probably didn't feel like a home at all for him.

"Listen." Jackson held the book up and read out loud. "'The ancient Egyptians believed in an eternal afterlife and, in fact, spent their entire lives preparing for it. They believed that the material world was a short but necessary step in preparing a person for Eternity. Mummification rituals, therefore, were an attempt to preserve the body for use in the afterlife, because without a body to dwell in, the soul would be lost.'"

Erik did not respond right away. His tongue peeked from the corner of his mouth. He was concentrating. Nipples were a mystery and always difficult. Fingers and nipples — they were the hardest.

Jackson looked at his friend and tried to figure out what was going on inside his head. Was he sad? Was he embarrassed, knowing that everybody was probably talking about him and his family all the time behind their backs? Jackson's father said that Erik's parents split because Erik's dad had ditched his family to move in with a younger woman named Mallory or something weird like that (Jackson could never hear the name clearly, since his dad lowered his voice whenever he talked about Erik's parents). Jackson's father knew the woman from when he had worked as a realtor at Century 21 in Portland, which was after he lost his job as a bailiff and before he got hired on at the travel agency. She had a bit of a reputation, Jackson's dad said once, perhaps a little louder than he'd intended. Jackson's mother had given him one of those disapproving looks.

"I don't get it," Erik said, finally.

"Don't get what?"

"How the body was supposed to, like, live in the afterlife. I mean, clearly they must have seen that dead people don't move or eat or anything. They could see that dead bodies never went any place on their own. Unless they're zombies, of course." Erik laughed, then looked at Jackson. "Do you think there was zombies in ancient Egypt?"

"Aliens and zombies?"

Erik laughed and shrugged. "I don't know."

Erik went back to his drawing and Jackson tried to get back to his book, but Erik's question hung in his mind. He had a good point. How was the body supposed to live in the afterlife? Maybe it was just like the Egyptians *knew* that dead bodies stayed dead and didn't actually go to the afterworld, but that the *idea* of the bodies continuing on after death was important to them. The idea of something is different from the thing itself, but can be just as real in its own way. Jackson looked at Erik. He wanted to see if his friend looked any different since his parents had split. It struck Jackson as funny how your whole world could be destroyed, yet on the outside, you appeared to be not different. It was almost like how the Egyptians prepared bodies for the afterlife, but in reverse. Instead of everything being taken out of your body so it could live forever in the spiritual world, everything can be taken from inside your emotional world, but you still live on in the real world as if nothing has happened.

Jackson stared and stared, but Erik did not seem any different. He looked up suddenly and caught Jackson looking at him. They held eye contact for a few seconds, and Eric didn't smile or anything; he just had a serious face and looked maybe a little sad and also kind of how you look when you look at a girl you like. Jackson looked back and smiled. He kind of knew that Erik had a man-crush on him and he kind of liked it. You can love people and not be in love with them; it probably wasn't gay. It was probably just a normal thing.

Caroline brought in some peanut butter and banana sandwiches, a bowl of Goldfish Crackers and a plate of raw veggies: carrots, broccoli, cauliflower.

"Don't forget, Jack; you have to finish Mrs. Wallace's garage today."

"It's raining, Ma." Jackson did not look up.

"It's *always* raining. Come on, honey, she's a nice old bird. She's just a little lonely. She's all by herself in that house since Mr. Wallace, you know, died."

Jackson picked up a sandwich and took a bite, without removing his eyes from the page. "The Egyptians believed that everyone had basically three souls. The *Ka,* a kind of duplicate of the body, the *Ba,* a kind of ghost that could come back from the across the River of Death and visit the mortal world, and *Akh,* an immortal soul that was forged after *Ka* and *Ba* united in the afterlife."

"I would like three souls" Erik said. "That would be cool."

"Ya. Even one soul that lived forever. Even one soul would be good, especially if you knew for sure you had it."

Erik put down his pencil and leaned back in the chair, smiling. He must have thought the picture looked pretty good.

"If I had a band, I'd call it IUD," Erik said. He picked up a sandwich and started tearing off the crust. "IUD'd be perfect."

"If I had a band I'd call it The Egyptian Book of the Dead."

"Na. It's too long. Would never fit on the cover."

Jackson didn't know how to respond. For a moment he considered the possibility that he — Jackson — had been a Pharaoh in a previous life, if such things as previous lives actually existed, all the time supressing the urge to lean over and crumple the drawing Erik was working on into ball and say something cruel about his parents being almost divorced.

He shifted his chair slightly and took another bite of the sandwich.

"Still," he said, after considering all the options, "the Egyptian Book of the Dead; it's a great name for a band."

Track 1: Ecstasy

Sometimes Diane liked to take E and dance for hours. She liked how it made her feel, how everyone was nice to her, how she was nice to everyone. She liked how it made the colours look different. It was hard to describe. Colours *looked* brighter. Jasper called E laundry detergent for your brain.

She'd met him at a rave at a warehouse near the Beaches. Sometimes she thought she was too old to go to raves, but once she got there and took some E she always had a great time. She was only in a bra and shorts and was telling everyone her name was Kaylee because when she closed her eyes one time she saw the name Kaylee in her mind spelled out in flashing **"Kaylee"** fireworks. Her hair was wet with sweat and beer, and she saw Jasper dancing with another cute guy who turned out to be his brother.

"You should totally be on TV," Jasper said, that was the first thing. No "Hey." Just — "You should totally be on TV."

She said, "You should be too, you totally could be. Or in a music video."

"I'm in a band," he said. But he really didn't need to. Diane already knew it. All the guys she was attracted to — Bird's dad, Mose's dad, everyone — were in bands; it was like she had a migratory instinct for musicians.

They danced together for hours, then Jasper went away to pee. He didn't return for a long time, and later

Diane saw him making out with some girl by the DJ booth. Diane didn't feel mad or jealous. She closed her eyes and saw neon snakes writhing in time to the music. Later, when Jasper came back and they were dancing with a group of people, he told her he loved her. They made out quite a bit, and she even let him slide his hand inside her bra even though there were people all around. His touch was magical, like his fingers had fingers.

They took a taxi to her apartment and they had a shower together, and every drop of water felt like a splash of music on her skin. And she took him in her mouth and even though he was soft it was the most erotic sensation she had ever had, something beyond sex, and they had stayed like that for what might have been hours; Diane on her knees, the shower, now cold, a thousand separate drops, each with its own weight and tone as it broke against her back, Jasper inside her, soft like a tongue, and rubbing shampoo in her wet hair. He said he loved her over and over again, calling her Kaylee just like the fireworks had said.

Track 2: Trick or Treat

"Just because someone doesn't have a lot of money doesn't mean they are lazy or stupid," Lenny said, which was funny in a way because, even though Diane agreed with what he said, Lenny could sometimes be the laziest and stupidest person you'd ever met.

Lenny was standing on the small balcony smoking some medical marijuana, still in bare feet even though big flakes of snow were falling. He was wearing a pair of plastic devil's horns on his head. Diane was tying up the back of Birdy's Spider-Man suit. He was pulling away, already ready to go. She was dressed like a sexy witch, with spiderweb stockings and leather boots, and a sexy little witch's hat. She always dressed like a sexy witch on Halloween.

Lenny finished the joint and came in from the cold and stood in the middle of the living room, leaning with both hands on his cane. Lenny owed the government twelve-thousand dollars in student loans. He'd had the bright idea of enrolling in Humber College, applying for a loan, then dropping all his classes. That way he had money and a library card. He did that for a few semesters, till the college caught on. Now the government wanted him to pay them back, and he was arguing with them, saying he shouldn't have to since he never finished college.

"Just because someone's not a millionaire doesn't mean you can walk all over him."

She'd never hear the end of this one.

At first Diane'd thought Lenny had a crush on her. He was always over at her place, just kind of hanging out. But he never once hit on her. So then she decided he was gay; you never saw him with a girl and he hung around a lot with his best friend Oliver, who was an esthetician and very effeminate. But now she just figured he was one of those guys who'd had his heart broken once, a long time ago, and never gotten over it. It's funny how one small thing could change a whole life. That was why he had all the medical problems, things with his back and stuff. He needed someone to love him and take care of him, even if it was just doctors and pharmacists and physiotherapists.

"I don't think Mosey-Posey will wake up." Little Mose was asleep on the couch, still in his panda bear costume.

Birdy was running to the door, shooting invisible spiderwebs from his wrists.

Diane stopped at the mirror in the hall to add a cute little witch's mole to her cheek with an eyebrow pencil.

"Thanks for looking after Mose, Lenny. We won't be long." She smacked her lipsticked lips. But Lenny was already on the balcony, lighting up another medicinal joint. Snowflakes were falling around his head and Diane somehow knew he would stay this way for the rest of his life, never really happy because he would never allow himself to be unhappy.

"Where's my broomstick, Birdy? Birdy, slow down — Mommy needs her broomstick."

But Birdy was already in the hallway, banging on the neighbour's door, uttering a vague and unintended threat, standing with his pillowcase open, waiting for some candy.

Track 3: Cause = Time

Diane was there the night the guy from the record company showed up. He talked to the band between sets and said he loved their music and wanted them to come in and cut a demo. He was too tall and too skinny and wore a too tight T-shirt that read *Cause = Time* and made him look older than he was, and not, as he probably intended, younger than he wanted to be.

The band was called Life Before Video and they could really rock. Jasper played the bass and sang some of the songs. He sang in a high voice — almost falsetto — like a girl, but not like a girl. It sounded very hot, and because he was so goddamned cute, even hotter. Jasper was three years younger than Diane. He had long brown hair and sexy big lips, almost like a girl. Diane thought he might be Icelandic, and asked him if he was Icelandic on their very second date. But he said, "No, Irish. Irish as Paddy's pig."

"What does that mean, 'Irish as Patty's pig'?"

Jasper shrugged and slid his hand down the back of her pants. "It means I like your ass."

Jasper's brother Johnnie played drums — a very tight rhythm section. Johnnie was a bit of an asshole, though, very high on himself. He'd hit on Diane already a couple times, but Jasper laughed it off and said his brother was just fucking with her.

The gig was interrupted when somebody threw a bottle of Wild Turkey and it hit Johnnie in the head. Knocked him out cold. He had a huge cut on his forehead and was bleeding all over the place, and Jasper went into the crowd to get the guy who threw the bottle and was taking a real shit-kicking when Diane took off her shoe and started hitting the guy over the head with it. Soon the bouncers were there, grabbing people, and they took the guy who had thrown the bottle away in one direction and Diane away in another.

Jasper had to come to the back door to get them to let Diane back in, and she had to spend the rest of the night in stocking feet because she'd broke the heel clear off her shoe. But that was okay, because she liked dancing in her stocking feet, and she liked how, when Johnnie came to and they were able to resume their set, Jasper looked right at her when he sang. It was a perfect night and

Diane didn't even mind when the guy from the record company came and started dancing with her and, later, how he put his hand on her ass and tried to feel her up. His aftershave stung her eyes.

"You're a good dancer." They were just a few feet from the speakers, and the guy from the record company had to yell to be heard. "Are you with the band?"

Diane shook her head. "No," she yelled back at the guy from the record company. "I just really like their music."

Track 4: Peppermints

Frank seemed agitated. His hand trembled slightly as he fidgeted with the BiC lighter.

"I've really got my shit together," he said, and when he smiled, Diane could see a thin green film on his teeth.

Her dad only saw her when he wanted something. Last time he'd asked her for coffee, he'd tried to borrow fifteen hundred dollars, almost half the money she'd inherited from Nana.

"You had your shit together a lot of times, Dad."

Frank lowered his head and said something that might have been *This time is different.* Then he lifted his head. "I haven't had a drink for three months. September 6. Mark it on your calendar." Frank smiled again and tried to pick up his spoon to stir his coffee. It took a couple tries, his hands were trembling so much, but he finally got it.

Dad had been in and out of her life since forever. Even before her parents split, Dad was away most of the time. Rosie wouldn't say anything about where he was and neither of the kids would ask. It was just easier without him around.

"Any plans for Christmas, Di?"

"Nothing special. Lamark will take Birdy; I'll probably make a turkey."

Maybe that was it? Maybe he was trying to wangle an invitation for Christmas dinner? But he was always at his worst on Christmas Day. One year, he'd woken up angry and had taken all the presents from under the tree and locked them in his room. Another year, Diane and her baby brother Sean found him passed out in the living room. He'd somehow knocked the tree down and was lying on top of it. He was too heavy for the three of them to move, so they just waited it out. They didn't get to open their presents until almost noon.

There was a long silence.

"They enrolled me in a program. It's really good. Out-patient, which is good, because it means I can sleep in my own bed at night."

Diane nodded. Frank waited.

Eventually, he excused himself to go to the bathroom. He was in there awhile and when he came out, Diane could see it right away. His eyes had that glassy look. Frank had an amazing capacity for alcohol. She had seen him drink a forty-pounder in under two hours. He'd been in the can for maybe five minutes, more than enough time for him to polish off a mickey.

He was smiling a lot when he sat down, and his hands had stopped trembling. He definitely had a buzz on. He said he loved her a couple times and told her how glad he was to be sober and how living one day at a time made a big difference to his outlook.

"It seems such a small thing, a little adjustment..."
He was already starting to slur his words.

He told her he had to go, he had an AA meeting at the downtown Y in an hour, he said, and didn't want to be late. He asked if he could borrow ten bucks for the subway and some gum. Diane gave him twenty. She knew he would use it to buy alcohol, but alcohol was the only thing in the world he truly loved. Alcohol was his mother and father, his wife, his son, his daughter.

"You're a good kid," he said, taking the twenty-dollar bill and folding it in half before putting it in his shirt pocket.

He hugged her just before he left, and was almost to the doorway when he stopped and turned around.

"I almost forgot; I got these for the boys." He gave her a handful of peppermint candies that had obviously come from a candy dish in some restaurant or doctor's office. He turned to go again, then turned back one more time to take a couple peppermints from Diane's hand.

"One for the road, kiddo," he said, and reached out to scruff her hair, but she got out of the way just in time.

Track 5: Krystal Kleer

Diane met him in the Bloor subway station. He just came up to her, an old man really, in a trench coat and a toque. He gave her a card: *Harold Murray — Krystal Kleer Photography.* He told her he'd been to the Playboy Mansion in New York City.

She knew it was sketchy, but she could take care of herself. And: two hundred dollars for a couple hours' work? She could use the extra money.

The place looked legitimate enough. It was a real studio and not just some room in the guy's apartment. It was an old brick building, and the room was very large and had exposed brick walls everywhere and skylights that made it seem like something you'd see in a movie. Harold had lots of photographic equipment and different kinds of lights and screens and backdrops. There were some old-fashioned couches and a couple big beds.

Harold was dipping a teabag in and out of a cup. Diane could see the steam rising, and somehow, the fact he was drinking tea, and not coffee or a pop, put her at ease. People who drank tea were generally nicer, more reflective.

There was another girl there, Carla. She was blond too, but not real blond. Diane was not surprised to see her, even though Harold had not mentioned that there would be another girl there.

"I'm not going to do any girl-girl stuff," Diane said right off the bat. Carla was sitting on a big armchair by the grated window. She was holding a fashion magazine and did not look up.

Harold shrugged and kept dipping his teabag. "You don't have to. *Playboy* likes girl-girl stuff, though. So if we shoot some, it just means we've got a better chance of getting noticed."

To his credit, he'd been really upfront. When he introduced himself at the subway station, he'd said that he was a photographer who had had stuff in *Playboy* and *Penthouse* and *Scientific American* and that he wanted to shoot her nude. There were no guarantees *Playboy* would publish the pictures, he said. But he said she had a fresh quality that *Playboy* liked. That was his word: *fresh*. He would pay her two hundred dollars: there could be thousands more, though, if *Playboy* was interested. But again: no guarantees.

"In the old days, we never had to shoot girl-girl stuff. *Playboy* wouldn't touch it. But, you know, it's hard to compete with all that garbage on the Internet."

Harold was very polite. He gave them terry-cloth robes to wear and offered them their choice of Perrier or fruit juice. Harold spoke very calmly and spent a lot of time adjusting lights and looking into his camera from various angles. He had an assistant, who he introduced as Michael. Michael stayed in the background and tried to be invisible. Harold would say things to him like "We need a barn door on three, Mike" and "Try a blue gel on two." While the words didn't necessarily make sense to Diane, they made her feel more at ease.

Diane and Carla lay on a bed with white sheets and lots of big white pillows, like in a hotel. Harold wanted them to be close to each other, but they didn't really have to touch each other or do anything. Diane didn't mind lying beside Carla. She was very warm, like a space heater, and smelled like flowers and nail polish. At one point, Gordie sprayed a fire extinguisher and the area filled with smoke and it smelled even more like a hair salon. Harold had Carla spread her legs and Diane kind of kneeled over her privates. Carla was completely shaved and her lips were flushed and Diane got a little turned on. Harold asked Diane to lean down some more and pretend to go down on Carla.

"Just close your eyes and think of all the money you'll make if *Playboy* likes what we're doing."

Diane didn't need to close her eyes and she didn't care

to think of money she knew she'd never see. She'd been to New York City a bunch of times, and didn't need to think of New York City, and didn't need to think of Playboy Mansions because she already knew that the Playboy Mansions in real life were not much different from the Playboy Mansions in your mind.

"Just a little closer, hun. Look like you're getting into it, Carla, like you're just about to, you know, cum."

Carla put both hands on Diane's head and ran her fingers through Diane's hair. Diane moved her face closer to Carla's privates and looked up. Their eyes met for a second and that's when they lost it. They both started laughing and couldn't stop and even eventually Harold started laughing too until he had to put the camera down and bend over because he was laughing so hard. Harold had to give everyone a break. He was smiling when he called them back a few minutes later, and even after Gordie sprayed the firehose, Diane could still hear Harold laughing, quietly, through the haze. It almost made her laugh again too.

Track 6: OxyContin

Diane and Jasper found Johnnie passed out on the bathroom floor. He had taken some oxy and drank a couple beers. There was a half-empty bottle of Robitussun DM on the counter. Jasper tried shaking him and yelling his name, and even splashed water on his face. You could see Johnnie's chest going up and down so you knew he was alive. Diane opened one of his eyes with her fingers: his pupils were pencil-tip dots.

55 •

"What should we do? What should we do?" Jasper said, and Diane realized that, even when he was stressing out, he sounded musical.

The ambulance guys came and crouched over Johnnie. Jasper had taken the oxy container, the half-empty bottle of cough syrup and the empty Molson's cans out of the bathroom, even though Diane told him not to. The younger ambulance guy, with the moustache and the Tigger tattoo on his forearm, asked a bunch of questions and basically did the same things Jasper and Diane had done. He shook Johnnie and called his name. He checked Johnnie's breathing. He opened his eyes and looked at Johnnie's pupils.

"How much oxy did your brother take?"

Jasper shrugged. "A couple tabs, I'm gonna guess."

"Did he hit his head or anything when he passed out?" The older ambulance guy was bald and short, and had a kind of cheerful look on his face. Diane figured he was the kind of guy who'd be making jokes all the time.

"I don't know, man. We just found him like this."

They wrapped Johnnie in blankets and put him on the stretcher.

"Are you gonna pump his stomach?" Diane asked, and the older ambulance guy laughed.

"If your grandma ran the hospital, everyone would get their stomach pumped," he said. Just for a moment, Diane felt stupid.

"Is your brother depressed?" The younger ambulance guy was adjusting the stretcher while his partner set up the IV. Jasper shook his head. And in the ambulance on the way to the hospital, Diane told Jasper that he shouldn't have lied, that the ambulance guys were only trying to help. Jasper acted like he didn't know what she was talking about.

"Johnnie is unhappy all the time," she said.

"Awww, that's just Johnnie. He's a drama queen."

Jasper got his cell out and took a picture of his brother on the ambulance stretcher. He showed it to Diane.

"Johnnie's got problems," she said.

Jasper nodded, then posted the pic on his Facebook page. "Everybody's got problems, baby."

He put his arm around her, but she didn't feel like snuggling in closer. She could still smell the cigarettes and beer and pepperoni pizza on his breath.

He looked at her and smiled, then took another picture of Johnnie.

Track 7: The Megalodon

Lamark was supposed to meet them in the food court in the basement of the mall. He was late, as usual, and he didn't have Birdy with him.

"I thought you had him."

"I left him with you, Lamark," Diane said. "Fuck."

Lamark was in town for a gig. He played drums for a jazz singer who was big in Montreal and Los Angeles. She toured all the time, taking Lamark to festivals and soft-seaters across North America.

Diane tried not to panic. She tried not to think of the terrible things that could happen to a kid who got lost. She tried not to think of the kid the police found two days ago in a plastic garbage bag, at the mouth of the Humber River.

They agreed. Lamark would stay put in the food court, right in front of the New York Fries. Birdy loved New York Fries, so it's likely that's where he'd go if he went to the food court. Diane would go look around and try and find Birdy.

Diane went to Santa's Village and to the toy section in the Bay. She was starting to panic by now and was kicking herself for ever allowing Lamark to take Birdy. He was irresponsible. He couldn't help it, he just was. He wasn't stupid; both his parents were college professors in America. But he just wasn't on the ball. ADHD. It was her fault for trusting him.

He was almost thirty. He had dreadlocks and wore one of those knitted Rasta hats all the time, even though he wasn't Jamaican. He wasn't even really black. One of his grandparents was black, which made him only a small part black. But he liked to talk like he was from the ghetto or something and when he met real black guys he would be all over them and call them bro and try so hard to be their friend that you knew he wished, deep down inside, that he was really black like them.

Diane looked in a store called Toys Toys Toys. Birdy was nowhere to be found. But she did see a giant stuffed panda bear on sale for forty-five bucks, and made a mental note to come back once she had some money and buy it for Mose.

There was a security guard standing outside Toys Toys Toys, and Diane went up to her and told her that her seven-year-old was missing. The security guard was about Diane's age and seemed very sympathetic.

"Kids go missing here all the time," she said, putting her hand on Diane's arm. "Don't worry, okay? What's his name?"

"Bird."

"Bird? Like, 'bird'?"

"Yeah. Bird, like the jazz musician."

The security guard asked Diane to describe Birdy. She showed him a picture on her cellphone. She told the guard that he was wearing a Spider-Man winter coat and red mittens his Nana had made.

The security guard turned her head and spoke to someone on her walkie-talkie. Diane tried to listen in, but couldn't follow the conversation. Finally, the security guard turned back.

"Yeah, we got him. Follow me."

She took Diane down the service elevator and into an area at the very bottom of the mall. They walked up and down corridors and through several doorways, until Diane was completely disoriented.

"I'm glad I didn't have to find this place myself," she said.

Then the security guard opened another door, and there was Birdy, sitting at a table with two other kids, drawing. She called his name and ran over to him and hugged him and gave him a kiss. He kept drawing.

"Can you guess what it is, Mommy?"

Diane examined the picture. It was definitely some kind of animal

"A reindeer?"

"No. It's a megalodon.

"A megalodon? What's that, hunny?"

"A giant shark from dinosaur times. They were the biggest sharks that ever lived."

Diane nodded, and told Birdy it was time to go

She thanked the security guard who had helped her, and

thanked another security guard sitting behind the desk, who seemed to be in charge. He was an older man, probably about Diane's dad's age, and had on a Santa hat.

"Thanks for taking care of Birdy," she said to the older guy.

He smiled and said, "If nobody lost their kids, I'd be out of a job."

By the time they got back to the food court, Lamark was nowhere to be found. Diane was a little pissed, but not surprised. She bought Birdy some New York Fries and thought about checking her phone to see if she'd got a message from Lamark, but changed her mind.

"Where's Daddy?" Birdy asked, and Diane told him that his dad had a gig to go to, which wasn't exactly a lie. He looked like he was going to ask another question, but then he took a crayon out of the pocket of his Spider-Man coat and started drawing on the placemat.

"What you drawing, hunny?"

"A reindeer."

"Nice. We can put it on the tree so Santa can see it."

Diane held the corner of the placemat, so it wouldn't slide. She looked around the food court, but everything was cool. Lamark was nowhere in sight.

Track 8: Flowers and Lithium

They were broken up by the time the EP came out. It happened New Year's Day— the breakup, that is. They had been arguing a lot and New Year's Eve had been a disaster. The band was supposed to be playing a gig downtown and it got cancelled at the last minute. The organizers couldn't get the permit from the fire marshall. Everyone just wound up getting too drunk at Diane's place. Things had already not been going well, and she and Jasper barely talked all night. When she gave him shit for ignoring her, he got mad and walked away. He slept on the couch: Happy New Year.

The EP was called *Flowers and Lithium*, and there was a song called "Kaylee," just like Jasper said. She must have listened to it fifteen times. It was slow and atmospheric, and made her feel like crying, even though she wasn't exactly sad.

Did you trip on the colours when you met on the beach
Could you taste the salt in the cracks of his skin
Would you count the holes in the air between you
You forget that in people, Kaylee, don't you
You forget that in people, don't you

She sent him a text to thank him for the EP and the song, and the next thing she knew they were in bed. It wasn't like before, when the hours seem to slide into orgasm. It was urgent: not quite a race or a competition, but not quite mutual. Two people, not one.

Afterwards, they showered together, and Jasper washed her hair and even said he loved her one time.

"Why'd we ever break up? We should totally get back together," he said.

"We totally should," she said back, knowing they never would.

Later, when she listened to the song with Lenny, he asked her if she would get money if the song became a hit. She said she was pretty sure she wouldn't get any money, and besides, the song wasn't just about her, per se, but about anyone who had ever been in love and lost that love but still hung on to part of it, and about what you have to give up when you are in love and what you have to hang on to, and about how the world is just a series of random moments and how love is a series of random moments too even though when you are in love it seems not to be random at all, and about how even something small and simple can be beautiful or terrible if you take the time to look at it closely.

"You should talk to a lawyer, just to be sure. I'm just saying; Jasper'd never have written the song without you. It's like, he had to steal a part of you to write it."

But Diane wasn't really paying attention. She was listening to the song and feeling very happy, like almost religious, and feeling like crying at the same time even though she wasn't really sad, and singing along.

Did you measure the dust in the corner of his eye
Could you hear him breathe when the radio told you
He doesn't have to love you if you don't want to let him
You forget that in people, Kaylee, don't you
You forget that in people, don't you . . .

It was on January 22, the day of the feast of the blessed Laura Vicuña, that Isabel Soré stood on platform 6 at the Estación Barón waiting for her fiancé to arrive on the train from Iquique. Instead, she welcomed only a monogrammed valise and the news that Señor Guillermo Olavide had succumbed en route to what the attendant physician suspected was a pulmonary embolism.

Señor Olavide's body arrived in Valparaíso six days later, the diagnosis having been confirmed by Iquique's Chief Coroner Eduardo Vera, and Isabel Soré found herself emotionally and legally in a curious nether region, halfway between jilted lover and grieving spouse. The legal questions were

The Widow Soré

settled relatively quickly by the local magistrate, who determined, despite a counterclaim by Olavide's estranged nephew, that the intent of the betrothal constituted a valid and binding contract, leaving Isabel Soré de facto spouse and therefore heir to Señor Olavide's not insubstantial estate. Out of respect for the court's decision, Isabel Soré felt obliged to wear black and found the habit to her liking. And thus the local gossips came to refer to her as *la tordo*, while others quietly spoke of her, with stinging sincerity, as the Widow Soré.

Although Señor Olavide was an avowed freethinker (his will outlined no explicit interment instructions), Isabel Soré engaged Father Errázuriz to bury her fiancé with full sacrament and secured Señor Olavide a respectable plot in the ancient cemetery on the edge of Iglesia de la Matriz.

Two weeks after Father Errázuriz led the *misa de requiem*, with Isabel Soré weeping rich tears at the loss of her betrothed (and the prospect of perpetual spinsterhood), Señor Olavide's effects arrived in a grand truck. The driver was a beardless Italian who spoke passable Portuguese. He had driven straight through from Iquique and asked only that Isabel Soré sign the requisite in duplicate and provide him with some wine, bread and hard cheese — provisions, he explained, to tide him through the return trip that was to begin immediately.

Three dull workmen unpacked the truck, slowly arranging Señor Olavide's effects on the tiled terrazzo, adjusting and readjusting the pieces as if following some ancient code. They were household items mostly and included several wooden packing crates marked *Frágil* (which contained sublime delights: a small collection of Nadal porcelains; a set of Galway Crystal fluted wineglasses; an incomplete Royal Doulton English porcelain dinner service) and several rooms' worth of furniture, including a ponderous dining table, clearly of Spanish design and seemingly carved from a single block of walnut, a pair of Queen Anne sofas — the kind that had been fashionable in the north some years earlier — and a monk-sized brass bed embellished with florid scrollwork suggestive, to Isabel Soré's mind, of a certain distasteful femininity. She caught herself blushing.

The workmen stepped from foot to foot like tethered horses as Isabel Soré considered her unwanted bounty.

She faced two equally unsavoury choices: give up the modest apartment in Doce de Julio, inherited from her father, José Miguel Sebastián Martinez Soré, the distinguished surgeon, or sell Señor Olavide's personal effects at a price, given the urgency of the circumstances, significantly below market value. By nature a pragmatist like her father, Isabel Soré decided to abandon her home and took a larger apartment several blocks to the west, in a rather more modern building.

At first, she found her new quarters unsettling. She could not take her morning coffee on the balcony without hearing the unbearable chatter of the finches, plovers and starlings that engorged the myrtle-covered trees on the avenue below, while the apartment itself became overheated in the evenings as the sun set. Worst of all, the throbbing, anxious light from the lighthouse at Punta Ángeles, clearly visible from her sitting room, illuminated the walls at night and robbed her of her sleep.

But she soon adjusted to the peculiar dialect of her new home. The conversation of the birds helped alleviate the pangs of loneliness that had come to trouble Isabel of late, while the evening heat, she found, aided in the digestion; as to the beacon light, Isabel Soré found the electric pulses had a strangely calming effect on her nerves. Soon she was sleeping better than ever.

And so she settled into her little nest, and several months had passed by the time the Widow Soré turned her attention to the monogrammed valise. It was on the feast day of San Isidoro de Sevilla that she discovered a ring of keys in a small crate that had been set aside in the corner of the guest bedroom, home now to that vulgar brass bed. At first the key ring struck her as worthless (she had, of course, inherited no doors from Señor Olavide), but then she remembered: the valise! She extracted the case from its hiding place under her own bed and set it on her father's sturdy desk. Like Señor Olavide himself, the valise was a dignified piece of work. The casing was raw leather, black and spicy, most certainly Portuguese, with fitted-brass hardware, a leather grip on the handle and ivory accents on the hasp and feet. The initials *JMO* were engraved along the top edge in what appeared to be, to Isabel's untrained eyes, genuine gold leaf. Having never bought something so opulent, she could not guess at its value.

She tried one key and then another and then another, and had almost finished the entire ring before she found success. The key chunked into the hole awkwardly and she had to jiggle it a couple times before it finally turned. For the briefest of moments, this simple act brought a crude image to her mind. Isabel Soré pushed it from her thoughts and did not allow herself to become flustered.

She opened the valise to find that it was almost empty save for a pork sandwich, now putrefying in a shroud of wax paper, and a manila envelope labelled in Señor Olavide's baroque script: *Sra. Doña Fontecilla.* The envelope, however, was not addressed and contained no clues as to its purpose or destination.

Isabel Soré could only assume the package contained legal papers and that there was undoubtedly some urgency in their delivery. She set the envelope on the desk. The temptation, of course, was to unseal the package and see if the contents provided any information that might help her contact Sra. Fontecilla — an address or postal box, a business name, etc. But to open someone else's mail: was that exactly proper?

From the desk drawer she extracted the antique *corvo* (that had helped protect her maternal great-grandfather, Gaspar Juan Lopez Illuminani, during the War of the Pacific) and slit the envelope along its seam. With painstaking care she unsealed the package and found inside a mimeographed document, with a curious title capitalized and underlined at the top of the first page.

<u>PERTAINING TO THE MATTER OF THE INTELLECTUAL PROPERTY RIGHTS TO THE DOCUMENT HEREAFTER IDENTIFIED AS THE ENCYCLOPEDIA OF LIES ("ENCYCLOPEDIA").</u>

Isabel Soré read the heading once again, then turned to the first page of the document. She found a typewritten letter with an address in the top left corner along with an opening salutation — *"Querido Guillermo"* — and at the bottom, where one might expect a signature to appear, were the initials <u>DF</u>, capitalized and underlined. There were pages and pages of these typewritten letters, all following the same format, all opening with *"Querido Guillermo,"* all closing with the initials <u>DF</u>. Some of the letters were just a few paragraphs long, others ran several thousand words, but all of them indecipherable to Isabel Soré. Not written in Spanish or any other familiar Latinate language (her French was rather quite good; her Italian, serviceable), she could pick out the occasional word — a proper name, the odd Gaullism that had at some point migrated into foreign vernacular — but as to the sense of the thing, that was lost on her.

She set the manuscript on the desk and stared at the light that calmly blinked across the wall of the study. What was the proper thing to do? Seal the document back up and make an effort to forward it to the intended recipient? That seemed obvious, although, in truth, Isabel Soré allowed herself to be tempted by convenience. She could throw the pages in the fire and be done with the matter. No one had inquired toward the document; no one seemed to be missing it at all. Who knew what other unfinished business Señor Olavide had rattling around? If she opened this particular can of worms, surely others would follow — and how could Isabel Soré be held responsible for all that? A decision was made: a cup of coffee and perhaps a cinnamon biscuit, and then to bed. The fate of *The Encyclopedia of Lies* could wait until morning.

Isabel Soré woke the next morning with the vague feeling that she had some small but terrible business to attend to. And then she recalled: the document. Propping herself up on her pillows, she plunged into *Sotileza* in effort to put the whole matter out of her mind. But to no avail. She found herself distracted and read the same passage — a description of Andrés Bitadura's first encounter with the merchant Venancio Liencres — over and over again, without ever making sense of it.

Throughout the day, thoughts of the document kept jumping up like a rabbit in a pot. At the fish shop, the hand-printed sign advertising fresh sea bass, the price underlined for emphasis, brought the initials <u>DF</u> to mind. Later, while walking through the park, she heard a woman singing *"Mi Buenos Aires Querido,"* putting an undue emphasis on the word *querdo* each time in a manner that struck Isabel Soré as deliberate and bordering on mockery. It was crazy; she knew it. That afternoon, riding the Ascensor Artillería down from the hills, she saw a condor coasting in the distance on the thermal winds and found herself choked with emotion. The wings, it seemed, stationary as the bird glided past, appeared like an indecipherable letter in the sky.

That evening over tea, Isabel Soré tried to enlist the help of Father Errázuriz.

"You are familiar with German, Father?" she asked, offering him a slice of lemon for his cup.

He shrugged and rubbed his rough beard with the back of his hand. "Not so much."

"English? Can you read that, Father?"

"English, somewhat. One must read English these days to get ahead. But just so much." Father Errázuriz held his thumb and forefinger a half inch apart and smiled. Isabel Soré resisted the urge to lean forward and wipe the biscuit crumbs from his beard.

"You are asking, Isabel Soré, because..?'

"It's just — there are some legal matters pertaining to Señor Olavide's business accounts. I would like to return some documents to their rightful owner, but am having difficulty making sense of them, you see."

"They are in English, yes?"

"They are in something unfamiliar, Father Errázuriz. English, perhaps German; I cannot tell. But I feel obliged to — I don't know — find their rightful owner."

Father Errázuriz nodded deeply, to impress upon Isabel Soré that he understood, then he gently laid his hand upon her arm. "Let me have a look."

He reviewed the documents for a moment, clicking his tongue on the roof of his mouth, occasionally raising his eyebrows in an exaggerated manner that seemed to Isabel Soré almost comical. After a few moments, he peered over the top of the document.

"They seem like nothing, Srta. Soré. Not business at all. Insignificant ramblings. I wouldn't give them another thought."

He handed the manuscript back to Isabel Soré, who suspected, her hand trembling slightly as she received the document, that Father Errázuriz was not being entirely forthcoming with her.

"What is it, Father?"

He smiled and patted her hand. "It's definitely English, my dear, and it is beyond my limited means to translate completely. But as far as I can tell, these are scribblings; nothing; less than nothing. Put them out of your mind."

Liebert, the Jewish student, was less discreet.

"*Lettera d'amore*, señora; love letters."

The student kept a small room above the printers on Pedro Lagos and was rumoured to be fluent in seven languages, including Hebrew and Farsi.

"I could provide you with a line-by-line rendering, Señora, but I suspect that would make neither one of us happy. There is reference to certain intimacies…" Here his voice trailed off.

Isabel Soré stood with one hand on the manuscript, as if she was about to take an oath, and tried to appear unflustered by the student's news.

"I could read it more thoroughly if you like, see if I can tease out some information to help you track down the party you are seeking."

The student spoke with a Castilian lisp, which made the matter at hand appear even more unseemly. She took her manuscript and turned to go, and did not bother to insist when the student graciously refused to accept the negotiated fee.

Isabel Soré slept poorly that night. The beacon, which had provided such comfort before, seemed harsher, and she could almost hear the light as it scraped across the bedroom wall. When she fell into a fitful sleep, the light was there, not so much illuminating her dreams as dragging her across the edges of them. When she finally roused, she was surprised that the sun was high in the morning sky and that the time, according to the black mantel clock, was quarter past eleven. Perhaps it was an error? Had she wound the clock the night before? She could not remember, and just as she rolled over to try and go back to sleep, Isabel Soré remembered: *Doña Fontecilla and her damned letters!*

With great effort, she pushed her feet to the floor and sat upright. She smoothed the folds of the bedsheet with one hand as she let her imagination wander. He could, she thought, hire a private detective to track down this Doña Fontecilla and (knowing full well she would never execute such an unseemly plan) confront the woman with the letters, tearing them up in her face and littering her sitting room with the cold flakes of paper, turning the illicit words of love into a snowfall of nouns, verbs, flowery adjectives — Isabel Soré imagined the woman's prose to be both lurid and extravagant — and incessant pronouns. But neither flights of fancy nor confrontation were in her nature. Isabel Soré settled on strong coffee and buttered toast.

She had almost finished her small breakfast when the bell rang, and on opening the door she was surprised to find the Jewish student leering down on her, almost out of breath.

"I've had another thought," he said, as if their previous conversation had ended moments ago and not the night before. He had a wild look in his eyes and had not properly groomed himself.

Isabel Soré did not invite him in, wedging herself between the frame and the door. "Perhaps it would be more appropriate if we scheduled —"

"Maybe it's a story." Liebert was smiling broadly now, clearly delighted with his proposition.

"I do not follow you."

"The letters, you know: *The Encyclopedia of Lies*. It occurred to me that perhaps it is a work of fiction, a novel of sorts, and if this were the case, perhaps your husband —"

Isabel Soré let the error pass.

"— was providing legal advice of some kind to the author, copyright protection or some such thing."

"And what of it?"

"Don't get your feathers ruffled, Señora! I'm thinking that this news might be of some comfort to you, and am curious now as to the exact nature of this work."

Isabel Soré contemplated for a moment.

"The name itself seems a dead giveaway, Señora. It's not an encyclopedia at all, in any formal sense of the word, although in a certain way — prosaically — it is a compendium of sorts. Each letter is a kind of article, building to a general understanding of the subject."

"And that subject is?"

The Jewish student now drew silent, then spoke in a deliberate way that suggested he was choosing his words carefully.

"Why, Señora, this fellow, Guillermo; he is a most precious man."

The word *precious* stung Isabel Soré's ears, and she thought suddenly of the brass bed and its ornate flourishes.

"The name Fontecilla is not unknown in the literary circles of this country, Señora, and I must admit that I gave the document only a cursory read. Perhaps I should review it again and prepare a more formal translation. I would hate to see a work of potential literary merit overlooked."

Isabel Soré felt a rush of indignation and struggled to keep her emotions in check. "I am not in the habit of procuring pornography, young man, regardless of its literary merit. I consider the matter closed."

Of course, when it comes to the heart, it is one thing to shut a door and another thing entirely to keep it shut, and even as Isabel Soré bid the Jewish student good day, her mind fluttered with thoughts of *The Encyclopedia of Lies*. She realized that it was only a matter of time before she would contact Liebert and commission him to provide a full translation of the work.

It was barely a fortnight later when the Jewish student

returned to her home, the translation tucked under his arm. Isabel Soré was bathing and had to call down to her visitor from the sitting-room window. He waited patiently on her doorstep for her to dress and presented the document to her with a slight bow. He was not unhandsome, she realized. A little unkempt perhaps, and in need of a haircut and a shave, but he had fine features and a kind of masculine delicacy that some women found attractive.

"And the verdict?" she asked, trying now to sound pleasant.

The Jewish student shrugged. "It's rough, to be sure, and rather too —" here he searched for the right word "— *expressive* for some tastes. But it is not without a certain flow and narrative charm."

"Does it have, in your opinion, artistic merit?"

Liebert shrugged again, in an even more exaggerated manner, and smiled in a way that seemed to Isabel Soré rather engaging.

"Who can say? It is not a precise science, literary criticism."

"I suspect it is not a science at all, precise or imprecise. I'm asking, rather, your opinion."

Liebert bit his lower lip, and Isabel Soré understood that once again the Jewish student was choosing his words judiciously.

"The venerable Hillel maintained that the most effective lies are constructed almost completely from truth and that, while it takes many great truths to unfasten the simplest lie, the mightiest truth can be undone by the smallest untruth."

"Which is a long way to go without answering the question: are the letters, Mr. Liebert, real or are they mere fancy?"

At this the Jewish student laughed, and his joy stung her. Was he making fun of her lack of refinement? She had always been one to admire the arts, but had never taken the time to understand them.

Liebert seemed to sense her discomfort.

"I am laughing, señora, not at the question, but at the difficulties inherent in your question. I have not the insight nor the imagination to distinguish fact from fancy; I will leave that up to you."

He bowed again, but as he turned to take his leave, Isabel Soré found herself reaching out to him. Her hand barely glanced his elbow. He turned sharply, his face half-hidden in the shadows cast from the sharp street light. They did not speak; rather, Isabel Soré contemplated his black eyes as they tried to read her thoughts. *He does not have the Jewish nose,* she found herself thinking, only to realize that the tips of her fingers were already in the palm of his soft hand.

Liebert left before the sun rose, swearing obeisance and promising discretion. Isabel Soré barely roused. She had taken lovers before and did not doubt his sincerity; she was never one to let a young man disturb her sleep.

As to Liebert's translation of *The Encyclopedia of Lies,* the document remained on her father's desk, untouched and unread, for several days. It was not that Isabel Soré was not interested in the manuscript — she thought of almost nothing else — but more that she realized the next step was one from which there was no turning back. Once she read one word, she knew she would have to read them all.

She decided to take her time, setting aside half an hour before lunch each day, and in this manner completed the document — some sixty letters — by week's end. It was difficult going at times. The prose was rough and often stilted (although this could be, Isabel Soré supposed, the fault of the translator), and she skimmed over sections that were too explicit or absurdly emotive (Doña Fontecilla's fondness for schoolgirl excess was embarrassing and left the reader, at times, questioning the author's mental faculties). In the end, though, Isabel Soré found herself drawn into the work. The woman wrote with a certain energy and an eye to detail that engaged one. It was an old story — a chance meeting, illicit love, separation, despair and, ultimately, a reunification of star-crossed lovers. Even the final, tragic twist (the untimely death of Doña Fontecilla's Guillermo) was nothing Isabel Soré hadn't seen before. Still, there was something there.

As to the question of its veracity, Isabel Soré could not say. The letters seemed real enough, but the story was too calculated to be believed. Life, to Isabel Soré, was more a collection of moments than a logical unfolding of events. Even in retrospect, it is difficult to find structure in the catalogue of details that defines one's life. Certainly, God had his plan in place, but that plan was beyond the capacity of mortal souls to comprehend. Yet, in Doña Fontecilla's document, every action had consequence, every passing statement resonance; every nuance of thought or feeling rang with possibility. Any truth one could find in the letters was shrouded in artifice, to the point where the mere notion of truth no longer held any relevance.

When it came to assessing the artistic or literary merit, Isabel Soré found the encyclopedia sadly lacking. True, she did not have the refinement of those women who moved in Valparaíso's more cultured circles and therefore could not be expected to appreciate the subtleties of art (particularly modern art, which seemed to Isabel Soré to venerate obscurity as its highest aesthetic), but to her mind art should elevate the world in some way, make it better than it was, and should strive for a certain beauty of spirit and moral constancy. On these counts, Doña Fontecilla's document failed spectacularly.

One thing was clear, though: the Querido Guillermo of Doña Fontecilla's encyclopedia was not the Guillermo Olavide to whom she, Isabel Soré, had been betrothed. The man she knew had never worked as a *huaso* in the rough Chilean southlands, had never married (Doña Fontecilla's Guillermo wed, at the age of twenty-three, a police captain's daughter), was never arrested (the Capitán had used his connections in the Carabineros to have Doña Fontecilla's Guillermo unjustly detained on charges of bigamy), had not escaped from prison disguised as a Chinese butcher, had never hidden for six months among the Mapuche shepherds of Patagonia. Nor was Señor Olavide the kind of man to sire a son out of wedlock (the eventual meeting of the bastard son and his estranged father was one of the emotional highlights of Fontecilla's encyclopedia), or fornicate (as Doña Fontecilla described in lurid detail) like a dog on the moonlit grass beneath the clock tower, or swim naked with seven sisters in the Todos los Santos, or secretly fondle the daughter of the governor of Chacabuco as her parents, on their knees beside him, celebrated the Eucharist

Mass, nor bring another woman to her lover's bed, as Doña Fontecilla documents on several occasions. Isabel Soré's Querido Guillermo had never blinded a man in a knife fight (as Doña Fontecilla's Guillermo had done to a lover's cuckolded husband), nor escaped by bicycle, under cover of darkness, pursued by a mob of angry relatives and vigilantes, had never trekked across the Andes by donkey, and at great personal peril, to deliver a love letter for a dying compadre, and was unquestionably not the sort to impose himself on a grieving woman who had just received a final letter from her now-deceased lover. It was plausible, Isabel Soré supposed, that Señor Olavide had owned a stake in an Argentinean gold mine, but inconceivable that he had acquired his share, as Doña Fontecilla's Guillermo had, in a rigged poker game, and while Isabel Soré was certain that Señor Olavide knew his way around a firearm — he had had a passion for hunting and had kept a collection of antique military handguns in a glass case in his office — Isabel Soré doubted that he ever used those skills to shoot the eye out of an eagle in flight to win a ten-thousand-peso bet or to take out five banditos in a Bolivian mountain pass. And most certainly, Señor Olavide had died only once, although the manner of the death of Doña Fontecilla's Guillermo was remarkably similar to her own loss (Fontecilla's lover died on a train heading to an undisclosed city; the similarity ended there, though, with Fontecilla's Guillermo suffering a heart attack after making love — twice — to a prostitute in a hidden corner of the baggage car), a detail that so unsettled Isabel Soré that she required two glasses of her father's *pisco* to calm her nerves.

The days and nights wore on; sleep was lost on Isabel Soré. Her doctor advised strong lavender tea, and still she could only manage two or three hours of fitful rest a night. She began to dread the evening routine: supper alone on her terrace, an hour of reading or needlepoint, a hot bath with a glass of *pisco*, followed by two cups of fragrant tea. And then, a night alone on her hard bed, trying to blot out the lighthouse's impersonal heartbeat.

The train to Iquique was inevitable. She delayed as long as she could tolerate, waiting a full fortnight and then another before purchasing her ticket. She wired ahead to Sullivan, Señor Olavide's aging agent, and asked him to secure her a room at the Camino Real, a hotel with a reputation for being respectable without being extravagant. Sullivan met her at the station. He was impossibly stooped and when he took her suitcase he seemed almost ready to break in half. He was already chiding her for making the journey herself; as Señor Olavide's representative in Iquique, he was obligated and only too happy to tend to any business requirements that may have arisen.

"Besides, Iquique is no place for a single woman of standing. It may look like a modern city on the outside, but beneath the paint it's still an old mining town and as rough as the devil."

Isabel Soré dismissed his concerns with a wave of her hand. She had no love for Sullivan and his Irish manner and hoped to keep her business as discreet as possible. Toward that end, she had concocted a rather plausible story about having come to Iquique to track down a long-lost relative, her mother's cousin, but when she mentioned the name to Sullivan — "A certain Srta. Doña Fontecilla" — he seemed to stoop a little further, and paused. He peered up at her, straining his neck as far as possible, scrutinizing her face, it seemed, for any trace of — what? Anger? Indignation? Irony?

After a moment, Sullivan lifted his chin, as if to smile.

"Do you play poker?" he asked.

"What a curious question, Mr. Sullivan."

Sullivan laughed and nodded.

"I am a curious man," he said, and picking up her suitcase he set off again. "This way please, señorita. My people and I will be only too happy to help you find your missing relative."

El Camino Real was more rustic than Isabel Soré had hoped, but the room at the very back of the building was quiet and clean enough. She sat on the bed, intending just to rest for a moment and collect herself, and was engulfed in a fountain of eiderdown. When she woke up, the room was dark and a cool breeze was blowing through the open window. An electric light rattled on a lamppost outside her window as a distant concertina played a not unfamiliar melody. Some old folk song, another lamentation to love lost. Her stomach was unsettled, perhaps from hunger, and she thought of getting up to trouble the innkeeper for some tea and a light meal. But the music seemed to pin her to the bed and carry her away, and despite the nausea, she drifted off to sleep.

The search for Doña Fontecilla was over before it began. Isabel Soré received a note from Sullivan with her morning tea, informing her that he had sent his boy round to the City Registry, and that the young man had found an address for her "long lost relative" (a phrase which he had inexplicably underlined.) He identified an apartment at 27 Tarapacá, within walking distance from El Camino Real.

She was in no hurry to reach her destination and took the long way through the market, past the stalls selling fresh grapes, avocado, nispero and pulpy, bittersweet cherimoya, through the artisans shops that line Baquedano Street, stopping for a while at the Astoreca Palace to take in the flowering copihue, which were in full bloom and had wrapped the entire mansion in a shawl of green and red. She inquired about the guided tours. She read a brochure about the museum dedicated to the Santa Maria School massacre, an infamous moment in the country's history when striking sodium nitrate miners, along with their wives and children, their mothers, their aged fathers — 3,600 in all — were gunned down by government troops. She tried to imagine suffering and misery on such a grand scale, and thought of Sullivan's warning about the city and the darkness that lurked just beneath the whitewash.

It was quarter past eleven by the time she arrived at 27 Tarapacá. She hesitated before ringing the bell. Isabel Soré had not formulated a plan. She had of course fantasized about meeting Doña Fontecilla, but it was always an imperfect scene, a dream of a dream, that spun off in a hundred directions. She understood she wasn't simply returning legal documents; that task could have easily been completed without all the minor humiliations that accompany a long train trip. No, what she was trying to do was put her own mind to rest. Doña Fontecilla's documents had left her — like her statutory widowhood — in a curious position, fluttering somewhere between a

81 ·

constructed reality and pure fabrication and, frankly, she resented that Doña Fontecilla had imposed the image of the salacious Querido Guillermo onto her own memory of the sober Señor Olavide. Still, it was now clear to Isabel Soré, as she stood outside Doña Fontecilla's cracked mahogany doorway, that she had no idea what she wanted to achieve, and the recognition of this uncertainty momentarily thrilled her. She reached up and rang the bell.

Several minutes passed before the door was opened. A mestizo housemaid, straining under her own weight, invited Isabel Soré to enter with a wave of her tired hand. She tried to explain her purpose to the maid, who said nothing in return. Perhaps she was mute? Perhaps it was improper in Iquique society for a servant to speak to her betters?

It was a slow walk in silence up the steep flight of stairs that led to Doña Fontecilla's flat. Isabel Soré tried not to stare at the housemaid, who grabbed the rails with both hands, pulling her heavy body up a step at a time, her grey linen uniform folding like soft iron as she pressed her hips against the banister for support. A curious smell filtered down from the apartment, something both sweet and harsh: a mix of cherry blossom and chlorine.

The apartment itself left the impression of a moment frozen in time. The sitting room was stuffed with thick armchairs, the cushions ornately embroidered, and at the very centre, a red velvet settee draped in a curtain of Venetian lace, suggesting that no one had ever sat in it nor ever would. Five or six ceramic clocks, precisely synchronized, ticked away on the long mantel, while almost every other inch of the room was inhabited by a figurine, glass or porcelain, mostly of spritely children or animals in various states of repose. Birds were a popular theme: here, a Sierra finch nesting; there, an Andean swallow relaxing on a ceramic branch. There was an austral black-bird bathing itself in a mirror pond, a snowy plover peeking from a crack in the bark. Everywhere one looked in this silent, frozen aviary: a thrush or finch or siskin.

And sitting in a small, hard-backed chair, almost lost in the collection, a minute woman, almost impossibly old, her legs crossed, a thin cigarette perched on her richly painted lips, the ash ready to drop at any moment.

The old woman smiled and adjusted her thick glasses.

Isabel Soré tried to speak but could not. She did not know what she had expected — an aging vamp perhaps, an older Antoñita Colomé with a girdled waist and exaggerated bosom, someone clinging by her talons to the edge of youth? But not this, an antediluvian insect in a lemon-coloured dress.

"It's so nice to see you again, my dear," the old woman said, in a thick accent that might have been British or even Australian. The housemaid said something to the old woman, rather harshly, in a curious guttural language that Isabel Soré took to be English. Doña Fontecilla mumbled something back, then adjusted herself slightly, her smile even more broad. She took a couple small puffs from her cigarette, and when she removed it from her lips to exhale invisible smoke, Isabel Soré saw that the side of the woman's mouth drooped (a small puff of spittle was collecting there), and that the entire left side of her face seemed lifeless. She noticed too that the woman's left hand remained curled in her lap, inanimate.

The housemaid silently took Isabel Soré's hat and, through a series of mute tugs, directed her to a rigid arm-chair across from Doña Fontecilla.

Isabel Soré introduced herself, and began to explain her business, only to be interrupted by Doña Fontecilla shouting to her servant — "Bring our guest some ice tea, Majo!" — as if she had no awareness that Isabel Soré had been speaking.

Isabel Soré tried again, pulling a thick stack of documents from her satchel and arranging them on her lap. "I've come with news of Sr. Guillermo Olavide, Sna. Fontecilla. I am sorry to tell you that he has passed away."

She waited for the information to sink in. Doña Fontecillas sat motionless, the exaggerated smile frozen on her lips.

"He was your solicitor, correct, Señora Fontecilla? He was doing some business on your behalf?"

Doña Fontecilla blinked through her thick glasses and continued to smile politely. Suddenly she turned to Majo, still hovering on the edges of the sitting room, and spoke to her in English. Majo answered back, again sharply, and Doña Fontecilla paused before asking another question. Another pointed reply, then Doña Fontecilla nodded her head, as if the clouds were beginning to lift.

"Ah, Guillermo!" she said finally. "You've come for him, yes?"

Isabel Soré again tried to explain the situation, but Doña Fontecilla held up her forefinger to quiet her. With great effort, the old woman pushed herself to her feet and shuffled to a stack of photo albums on a shelf beneath the mantel. She selected one album and slowly turned the pages, all the while carrying on half a conversation with herself, drifting from English to Spanish and back again as the fancy struck her.

Finally, she found what she was looking for and hobbled her way back to the chair. As she sat down, Doña Fontecilla laid a cracked photograph on Isabel Soré's lap. It was a picture of a young *huaso* — with a beautiful, soft face and wide, dark eyes that immediately drew Isabel Soré in — his arm playfully around the neck of a horse. The animal seemed to be taking a bite out of the cowboy's Cordoban hat, much to the young man's delight, while another horse, a colt, had its head buried in the *huaso*'s *manta*.

"Guillermo," Doña Fontecilla said wistfully. "Querido Guillermo."

"I understand, Doña Fontecilla; your Guillermo was a very handsome young man. But I am here on other business. You had left some documents in the possession of my fiancé, the solicitor —"

"Querido Guillermo," Doña Fontecilla said again, now tapping the photograph aggressively with her finger. What was the old woman trying to tell her? Isabel Soré scrutinized the picture, looking for any trace of Señor Olavide in this young cowboy.

"Your fiancé was the *huaso*?" Majo asked from the shadows.

"No. She's mistaken. My — he was a solicitor."

"You must excuse Señora Fontecilla. Things confound her much of the time."

"Nonsense!" Doña Fontecilla snapped, drawing herself back in her chair, then speaking harshly to Majo in that language that sounded, to Isabel Soré's ears, like so many animal grunts. Majo gave as good as she got, and the angry exchange between the two women went on for some minutes before they both suddenly stopped. There was a long silence, then Doña Fontecilla relaxed and smiled again.

"Read to me," she asked, a certain urgency in her voice.

Isabel Soré was taken aback.

"Excuse me?"

"I am nearly blind, my dear. Please, open your storybook; read to me."

Isabel Soré recoiled slightly, then adjusted herself in her seat.

"These are personal documents, it's not appropriate that I —"

"Please, Señora, I implore you. Read to me."

Isabel Soré shuffled the papers in her lap. The sun was coming in a small window at the front of the sitting room, leaving long shadows on the wall and, across the alleyway, Isabel Soré could see an old man, a bachelor perhaps, watering a row of bougainvilleas in his window box.

"It's an extensive document, Señora Fontecilla; it would take me hours to read it — days!"

Doña Fontecilla leaned forward and patted Isabel Soré's hand. Her fingers were cold but surprisingly soft. "Not to worry, my dear. You've come such a long way, and we have all the time in the world."

The Widow Soré shuffled the papers in her lap, conscious of the old woman staring at her with those grasshopper eyes. She considered the option of escape. She could simply stand up and make her way back down the stairs and out into the hot Iquique sun. But she was neither graceless nor a coward and had quickly come to recognize that the game she had become entwined in could not be won or lost, only endured, and that any evidence regarding the true nature of Guillermo — whether he was one man or two, many or all — was not as important as the words each woman used to define their memories of him. In this context, the discovery of *The Encyclopedia of Lies* among Sr. Guillermo Olavide's working papers made sense. It was a legal document, of sorts, although presenting neither evidence of any sort nor argument of any substance. Rather, it was a clever puzzle, an exercise for those daunting, judiciously minded men with whom Señor Olavide associated.

Isabel Soré smiled and licked her finger, then turned to the first page.

"Pertaining to the matter of the intellectual property rights to the document hereafter identified as *The Encyclopedia of Lies...*"

At first the words came hesitantly, perhaps due to the inelegance of the translation, but also because Isabel Soré was sharply aware of the sound of each word as she uttered it. But as she moved through the story, the words took on a vitality of their own, until sentences were slipping from her mouth without conscious effort or even thought. As she continued reading, every detail, which should have by now been familiar, seemed new. Guillermo's childhood spent working in his grandmother's brothel — how could she have missed that on her first read? — emptying slop buckets and washing sheets to earn his keep, and the loss of his innocence, at age twelve, in the pigsty, to a mad cousin seventeen years his senior. The stories were both fresh and familiar, as if she were reinventing Querido Guillermo as she read, as if the words themselves were being written only as she spoke them.

Her mind wandered, first carried away by a glimpse of a tiger-striped butterfly — *Heliconius ismenius* — fluttering by the window, then to a herd of angular clouds grazing across the distant sky. And she continued reading for the matron, relating the particulars of Guillermo's flight through the temperate forests of the Rio Negro, pursued by German vigilantes, which culminated with him hiding out in a Carmelite convent (where he spent two nights and a day deflowering a dozen mendicant nuns before escaping through a secret passageway with the Mother Superior's blessing), lingering over the lurid description of Guillermo's liaison with a perfumed sodomite in a Buenos Aires' Turkish bath, and on through a litany of petty crime, misguided gallantry and sexual adventure, reciting from a place halfway between memory and invention, no longer thinking of another night of privations at the Camino Real or the long train ride ahead, from Iquique to Valparaíso, no longer bothered by Doña Fontecilla's exoskeletal smile or the ceramic decay that surrounded the old woman, or Majo's drawn, heavy, deathbed breaths and frequent grunts of disapproval. No. The Widow Soré drew her shawl tighter across her shoulders, licked her finger once again and turned to another page.

She could not say how long she read to the old woman. In the back of her mind, Isabel Soré fancied she would continue on until Doña Fontecilla capitulated, ceding all claims to the Querido Guillermo of their shared imagination. But eventually, as darkness ensconced the house, her voice grew raw and she stopped to sip the bitter tea Majo had provided, she realized that the weather-beaten nurse was soundly asleep in her chair. She turned to look at the ancient Doña Fontecilla, still balanced on the edge of her chair, the circle of red lipstick around her mouth now entirely smudged.

The two women considered each other for a moment, until Isabel Soré found herself opening her mouth to speak.

"We were engaged to be married, you know."

Doña Fontecilla's expression did not change. Her lips still frozen in that empty smile, her old eyes still magnified by her thick glasses.

"And I should say, Señora Fontecilla, I am with his child..."

It was an audacious statement, to be sure — rash and impetuous — and Isabel Soré had no idea why she felt the need to say it. Still, she felt a certain exhilaration as the words flew from her mouth, a quiet elation that intensified as she saw the smile on Doña Fontecilla's lips retreat, only slightly and only for the briefest of moments.

"It is a terrible scandal, I know, Señora Fontecilla, but I must admit, I am not ashamed. Señor Olavide was a decent man — a good, stable, decent man — and we were, as I have said, engaged to be married."

By now, Doña Fontecilla had regained her composure, and she slowly blinked those watery, dragonfly eyes.

"Querido Guillermo," she said, savouring each syllable.

It was then that Isabel Soré noticed that her hostess was still clutching the photograph of the young *huaso* in her twisted hand. The Widow Soré leaned forward and, while allowing her eyes to avert from Doña Fontecilla's animal gaze, she plucked the photograph from her hostess's talons.

Without a word, Isabel Soré tucked the photograph into her breast pocket and, collecting *The Encyclopedia of Lies* in one hand, stood to leave. She walked briskly, turning only briefly to wish Doña Fontecilla a good evening, before descending the stairs and letting herself out the door and into the gentle darkness of the Iquique night.

The next morning, Isabel Soré woke suddenly, feverish and thick with nausea. She vomited twice, once in the basin by the vanity, and again, as she was making her way back to bed, in the wastebasket by the small desk. For a moment, she allowed herself to think the worst — a typhoid outbreak in the saltpetre mines north of Iquique had been widely reported in the papers. But her stomach soon settled and she managed to enjoy a light breakfast: Swiss cheese, half an avocado, a slice of cold ham, toasted rye bread and black coffee topped with a dollop of *dulce de leche.*

Later, on the train to Valparaíso, the nausea returned and brought with it a tenderness in her breasts. Isabel Soré stayed in her couchette until the nausea passed, and by the time the train reached La Serena, her mind was made up: she would go home to settle her affairs, then take a trip to nurse an ailing aunt in Viña del Mar. There were some scandals even the Widow Soré could not weather.

She would return in the spring. Of course, she would have to endure the murmured slander of servants and old women, but Liebert's discretion had been bought and paid for, and she was certain that Father Errázuriz would provide his sanction. The child could be raised with the blessing of the church and state. Isabel Soré had even settled on a name: María Soledad, if it was a girl, after Isabel Soré's sainted mother; Guillermo Juan-Carlos, if the child was a boy, to honour both his father, the respected jurist Guillermo Olavide, who in his youth had worked as a *huaso* in the rough Chilean southlands, and his maternal great-grandfather, Juan-Carlos Emanuël García Soré, a decorated war hero and celebrated botanist, who served three terms as the Minister of Agriculture in Chile's Congreso Nacional.

Since its **"discovery"** almost ten years ago, the so-called Braşov *Moby-Dick* has created a stir within a small but impassioned cadre of Serbocentric literary enthusiasts. Granted, even within this limited group, interest is marginalized and largely the province of committed conspiracy theorists and plastografialologists. A small article in the *New Yorker*, followed by longer profiles in the likes of *Vanity Fair*, the *New York Review of Books* and the *Times Literary Supplement*, has cast the net further into the public imagination and nudged the manuscript into territory usually reserved for the classics of our literary canon (that being: books that are much discussed but never read). I hope that this volume, being the first English translation of the manuscript, will go a small way toward fuelling this interest and informing the discussion.

Preface to the First English–Language Edition of the "Braşov" *Moby-Dick*

That the original manuscript is extant (which is not always the case with controversial documents of this type), and has held up to some scientific rigour, has only enhanced the debate. Without question (to this observer's mind), the manuscript is a forgery. The fact that the paper stock is consistent with stock available and used by a number of underground Eastern European publishers operating around the alleged time of publication is moot: paper of such (relatively) recent vintage cannot be dated with any accuracy. Usually, researchers must rely on a watermark to establish stock dates, yet frequently, as in the case of the Braşov manuscript, no watermark is present. A clever forger need only find paper of the right vintage and locale (there are dealers in Asia and Eastern Europe who specialize is this), and they are set. Moreover, much has been made of the analysis of the ink used in the document, and the fact that researchers have established the presence of cedar-nut oil — which is very particular to Russian and Scandinavian printing presses at the turn of the century. This is a further fury that signifies nothing. Any good art supply shop in North America today carries such ink, or could get their hands on it in a matter of days.

More intriguing is the case of the attributed author himself, Uros Knezevic. It has been established with a fairly high level of certainty that a man of this name lived and worked in Belgrade during a period that roughly corresponds with that described in the Braşov *Moby-Dick*. That he lived briefly in the Canadian city of Etobicoke is also established. The (approximate) date of his death is not inconsistent with the Braşov narrative. More detailed research has yet to be conducted. But regardless, these facts neither prove nor even suggest anything. Both the Christian name and surname are fairly common throughout Serbic Europe, while Canada remains a regular destination for those trying to escape the ethnic turmoil that reached a peak in the late 1990s (but had been ongoing since, at least, the demise of the Austro-Hungarian Empire and resultant Baltic diaspora).

Limited debate on the "authenticity" of the manuscript continues. What we do know for certain is that it was purchased from an antiquarian bookstore in the Romanian city of Braşov by one Herta Pichler-Scheel, a respected Proust scholar who was, at the time, on sabbatical from her teaching post at Ludwig-Maximilians-Universität München (regrettably, Frau Professor Pichler-Scheel passed away during the preparation of this volume). Reports that the bound manuscript had arrived in Braşov by way of the Pavlov Museum in Ryazan are no doubt apocryphal, and were dismissed out of hand by the professor when I spoke to her earlier this year.

Until now, the manuscript has only been available in facsimile form, and the translation presents difficulties for the Western reader that go beyond the poorly rendered Cyrillic type. Although there is some idiomatic evidence to suggest that the author wrote the original draft in English (not to mention repeated references in the text to the "original" Kapitol Klassics — the name seems spurious — edition), the Braşov manuscript is in Russian and, further, appears to be a rather poor translation from Serbian (again, there is idiomatic evidence to suggest this, along with several phrases and passages in Serbian that give the appearance of having been overlooked by the editors and simply rendered untranslated). This tangled web proved difficult when it came to preparing and editing this first English edition of the work, and I find myself indebted to a vast team of translators. Particular thanks are due to Dr. Georges Bogolmov of Carleton University's Department of Slavic Studies, Sandra Urschel of the New York's Pratt Institute and, of course, the entire staff from the Department of Philology, Univerzitet u Beogradu. I would be remiss as well if I did not acknowledge the generous support of the National Council of the Arts and the Deutsche Forschungsgemeinschaft.

Throughout the editorial process I've tried to use as light a touch as possible. My goal was to be true to the original document, but this of course begs the question: which original? Given that the manuscript is likely at least two generations removed from that which was composed by the author, this was not always an easy dictum to obey. In the end, I erred on the side of clarity and simplicity.

The result, I hope, is a volume that not only satisfies the needs of serious academics, but opens up the Braşov *Moby-Dick* to a more general readership. There are delights to be found by both audiences, not the least of which is the central intrigue presented by the book: for if it is a fake (and surely it could be nothing otherwise), who wrote it and why did they go to such extraordinary lengths to perpetrate this fraud?

The answer is not found in this volume, but the question permeates.

Caroline wiped the bread crumbs from the counter with a wet cloth. She made a line of crumbs and swept them into her open hand, dumping them into the sink before giving the counter one last wipe.

It was one thing she couldn't stand: crumbs on the counter. It was visceral. It made her physically uncomfortable to look at them, she didn't know why. Maybe it was something she had inherited from her father? He would get angry if someone spilled a drink or made a sandwich and didn't clean up after themselves. Not just upset. Angry. He might pound the counter with his fist or kick the cupboard door. If he caught you doing it — leaving a spill or leaving crumbs — he would slap you on the side of the head, then stare at you with his hand out, as if he was going to hit you again. Getting mad

Crumbs

about spills on the counter. It was just one of the things about Caroline's dad; "tics," her mother called them. Caroline's dad had a lot of tics.

They say we marry our parents, so maybe that was why she had been attracted to Ray in the first place. He had a lot of tics too. Not crumbs-on-the-counter, but other stuff. His little obsessions, the things he needed to occupy his time: stamp collecting, compiling historic baseball stats, collecting vinyl bebop records, things not quite useless but as close as you could come without actually being useless. He had a temper too, Ray; not big explosive outbursts like her dad. More of a slow burn. Inward, not outward. And the drinking, of course. Caroline's dad had been a heavy drinker — he liked his rye — and, in the end, was rarely sober past noon. Ray was more subtle, and his drinking ebbed and flowed. Sometimes, it seemed like he would go weeks without taking a sip. Then she'd notice him spending more and more time in his "studio" — the spare bedroom in the basement where he kept his computer and stereo. He'd sit in there for hours listening to strange jazz music, staggering into bed in the wee hours of the morning. When she checked the studio, which she did every so often, she'd find empty wine bottles hidden behind speakers and underneath the small recliner (searching the studio was a kind of a ritual that both confirmed her suspicions that Ray was, indeed, off the wagon, and fuelled her disappointment, which, as her counsellor had pointed out only recently, was a kind of acceptance).

There had been times she had thought of leaving him, packing up some suitcases, throwing Jackson and Sarah in the car and getting out of Portland. But she never did. Some of her friends told her she was wrong to stay, but her counsellor supported her. She said that there was no right or wrong thing to do; life was a journey, the counsellor said, and she, Caroline, was on a journey just like Ray was on a journey and Jackson was on a journey and Sarah and everybody else. Life is an event — that was one of her counsellor's favourite sayings. It had a beginning and a middle and an end. It was dynamic. You couldn't judge your life or even come close to understanding when you were standing in the middle of it.

Caroline felt the cellphone vibrate in her pocket. She didn't check it. She didn't want to check it just yet.

She put the lid back on the peanut butter jar and put it in the fridge. Saturday was her day to clean up, do the laundry. She didn't mind it, really. She liked having a clean house — it took her mind off things to putter around and straighten up. She'd do one room at a time, and it never stopped surprising her how quickly you could turn a room around just by tidying it up a bit. One minute it'd be messy, the next, clean.

It worked both ways, of course, the whole marry-your-parents thing, and if she had married Ray because he reminded her of her dad, who did she remind him of? Not his mother, surely. Larraine was a real piece of work, a real worrywart, a hypochondriac, literally. Munchausen's disease. This wasn't just speculation on Caroline's part. Ray's sister Cheryl had talked to her about it. It seems Larraine was being regularly admitted to the hospital in Milwaukie, complaining that her heart was palpitating and racing. It was a real medical mystery; the doctors couldn't figure out what was wrong. But obviously something was happening because they were running all these tests and seeing how crazy her heart was acting.

The last time she went into Emergency, though, one of the nurses was moving Larraine's coat and a bottle of caffeine pills fell out of the pocket. Turns out, she was taking like fifteen, twenty pills a day to make her heart act up. At first, Larraine had denied that she was taking the pills, but she broke down when one of the emergency room nurses chewed her out for wasting valuable hospital time and resources that could have gone to help someone who was really sick.

Why she did it, of course, was anybody's guess. But Caroline figured that Larraine wanted the attention, and that was both sad and frustrating, because both Caroline and Cheryl bent over backwards to do stuff with Larraine, keep her busy and engaged. But there were deeper forces at work, she supposed; her mother-in-law's parents had been no great shakes either.

Caroline got the scrub brush and small bucket out from under the sink. Maybe she was a little like Larraine. You can never really see yourself that clearly. Everybody seeks attention in their own way. Maybe being invisible was her way of seeking attention. Maybe being a quiet shadow was her Munchausen's? Caroline started wiping up some mud stains on the kitchen floor with a rag and spray cleaner, then realized just how dirty the linoleum really was. It wasn't a smart choice on their part, the linoleum, especially in a city like Portland, with all the goddamn rain. But Ray really liked the simple pattern, and thought the flooring would complement the new cupboards nicely. But once the linoleum had been put down, they both realized it had a kind of bumpy texture that was a magnet for dirt.

She filled the bucket three-quarters of the way with hot, soapy water and got a dirty towel from the laundry. She had a system. First she'd spray an area of the linoleum with Mr. Clean. Then she'd scrub the area with soapy water, pushing down hard on the coarse brush with both hands. Then she'd wipe the area clean with the towel. You could see the difference right away, how much cleaner the newly cleaned area looked compared to the rest of the floor, and how the floor you thought was clean only moments ago was in fact soiled and dirty. Layers upon layers upon layers.

The phone buzzed in her pocket again. It was probably Ray. He was always all over her the day after he'd been drinking, apologizing, promising. He had made an appointment with the counsellor for today, which was a good thing, but she wasn't optimistic. He only made appointments when he was doing bad. She kept telling him that the time to go was when you were doing good, when you actually had the emotional wherewithal to do something positive. But he never listened, and she was tired of saying something to someone who didn't listen.

Caroline looked up. She could see Jackson and Erik working away. So serious. She hadn't liked this boy at first, Erik. There was something about him, like he was too polite. At first, she thought he was up to something. But then she realized he just wanted to be liked. Things couldn't be that great at home for him right now with the divorce and all that. She liked that he felt comfortable here.

Caroline thought to remind Jackson one more time. She didn't like to nag him. She preferred it if he took responsibility for himself. But kids seemed to lose their ability to concentrate the minute their hormones started kicking in. Boys especially. One day, it just happens. The hormones kick in and all of a sudden they start to smell bad and turn kind of stupid.

Besides, Mrs. Wallace could really use the help. That poor old woman, alone in that house of hers. She'd had a terrible run these past twelve months, really, and should have probably been in a proper seniors' residence where she could get the care and support she needed. But Mrs. Wallace had her stubborn streak. She'd probably finish out her days rattling around that big old house, alone. It made Caroline sad to think of that. The poor old woman, alone in her house, so alone, in fact, that she no longer knew she was alone. And that's how you end it, alone, so many defeats and compromises away from where you thought your life would be. She wondered, suddenly, if celebrities felt the same way. Did George Clooney ever feel like his life just never panned out the way he'd wanted it to? That'd be funny if he did. That would mean that no one's life, not even George Clooney's, can live up to the expectations that people have for themselves. Not that Caroline's life was all that bad. It's just, you grow up having an idea of what a marriage should be like, think that it's like two lives coming together and making one single life, somehow bigger, somehow better than the life you could have had yourself. But that's not necessarily the way it turns out.

Her phone was vibrating again. Caroline took it out of her pocket and turned it off. She plunged the scrub brush into the bucket of hot water. She would finish the kitchen floor and then move on to the upstairs bathroom. She was hoping that in a year or two they would have enough money to do a proper reno on the bathroom, put in one of those Jacuzzi tubs and a new vanity and sink. But for now, she'd give it a good scrubbing. It wouldn't be as good as new, but it'd be good enough.

I. Statement of the Problem

They were everywhere, hundreds if not thousands of them, speckling the kitchen counter and walls, basking in the tepid leftovers on the unwashed plates and bowls, sunning themselves on the wandering Jews, the devil's ivies, the long-leafed figs and the Madagascar dragon trees; they'd crammed the edges of Hector's water bowl like Japanese commuters, until Kyle had to move it outside and install a cat door.

Dissertation on the Reproductive Habits of Fruit Flies from the Mango Groves of Eastern Uganda

Nikki and Kyle had checked all the usual sources — the drainpipe in the kitchen sink, the trash cans in the pantry and washroom, the jungle of potted plants in the sunroom — and were no closer to discovering the source of the infestation, when Nikki, on a whim, decided to give the nursery a thorough going-over.

Baby Nkunda was asleep, his face turboted in a helix of blankets. When they'd first brought Nkunda home, his sleep position concerned them to no end. They researched the risks: adopted babies were seventeen per cent more susceptible to SIDS than non-adopted babies;

African-American babies (there were no statistics available specifically on African-born children) were four times more likely to suffer crib death than Caucasian or Asian babies; babies who slept on their stomach faced a higher risk (less than .2 per cent, but still) than those who slept on their backs. The fact that he was such a sound sleeper did not help ease their minds. For the first six months, Nkunda stayed in a crib in their room, as per the American Sudden Infant Death Association's recommendation, going down every night at eight o'clock and sleeping through until eight the next morning. They slept in fretful shifts despite Dr. Wasserman, the pediatrician, assuring them that there was no such thing as a "typical" sleep pattern for infants and that well-rested babies were at no greater risk of succumbing to SIDS than cranky, overtired ones.

"It's a blessing, really," the doctor told them. "You are the envy of ninety per cent of the parents I see."

Still, they would softly roll Nkunda onto his back every hour, only to find him curled up face down at the start of the next shift.

It didn't take Nikki long to find what seemed to be the source of the infestation: a mist of fruit flies hung over the deodorizing filter in the diaper bin lid. She lifted the lid to find a thick paste of flies coating the soiled and folded disposable diapers. *The motherload.* Some of the flies scattered as Nikki prodded their mass with the scouring pad, but most of them remained, congealing for warmth or comfort or sexual congress or whatever it was that compelled these creatures to do what they do. Nikki snapped the lid down, moved the bin to the back porch and gave the nursery — and house — a thorough cleaning.

But at dinner that night, they returned. First the odd fly appeared, strafing their spoons as they brought a helping of chicken stew to their lips. Then the flies were at it again, swarming around their mouths like frozen breath, hovering over the stew pot, patrolling the cornbread moonscape, imperceptibly weighing down the napkins. Nikki gave up trying to feed herself and focused on keeping flies away from Nkunda's eyes and mouth. The fruit flies covered his little fingers and baby spoon; they collected in the moist folds at the back of his neck.

"This is insane," Nikki called to Kyle, who had, by now, got the vacuum cleaner out and was tracking down fruit flies with the intensity of a Kalahari huntsman.

"What?"

"We need to call the pest-control people again."

Kyle nodded, but was not paying attention. He was on his hands and knees, peering into the gap between the refrigerator and the sideboard, slowly deploying the vacuum hose.

And that's when Nikki noticed something odd; they appeared to be congregating by the side of Nkunda's head, the flies, lining up almost, in orderly holding patterns, and just as one flew in the infant's ear, another flew out. Nikki leaned closer to get a better look.

"Kyle? *Kyle?*"

II. Review of the Literature and Research Questions

"They are children, these Americans. They wear jeans to work: *jeans!*" Betty Obote sat behind a stack of manila file folders, carving the flesh from a heel of mango with an aluminum spoon. "They are infants, Mildred, big infants who need to be taken care of."

"No refunds, Betty — did you tell them that?" Mildred Kamugasa, who was crafting an email to an agency in London, England, did not look up. "Tell them to read the warranty."

"No refunds, girl..." Betty Obote laughed and leaned back in her chair, allowing the breeze from the ceiling fan to cool her face. She read the letter one more time, every once in a while waving her hand unconsciously at the fruit flies circling the discarded mango skin.

"Don't they know we have better things to do?"

"Like you said, Betty, they are children. They only think of themselves."

"There are two million orphans in this country, Mildred. Do they think it's a department store? You just come and buy a child and take it home, and if it doesn't fit with the decor, you exchange it for another?"

Betty Obote folded the offending letter in half and got a container of dental floss from her drawer. She had beautiful teeth, and flossed and brushed them several times a day.

"I need another word for *temporary*, Betty." Mildred Kamugasa had paused mid-type, her fingers arched over the keyboard.

"Hmm. *Time-limited?*"

"No. My brain is stuck. More of a legal term."

"*Interim?*"

"That's it girl: *interim.*" Mildred Kamugasa talked silently to herself as she typed, trying to weigh the impact her email would have on Mr. Anthony DeLuce, solicitor for the Families First Agency, 66 Newhams Row, London.

"Everybody wants to ignore the residency requirement, Betty Obote. You would think Mr. Anthony DeLuce would know better."

"It's a wonder we still *have* the residency requirement, Mildred."

"The judges need their money, girl." Mildred Kamugasa rubbed her thumb and forefinger together. "You get rid of the residency requirement, that's money out of a lot of pockets."

"They'll find a new way to get their pound of meat, Mildred, don't you worry. The judges, they are good at that." Betty put her hands on the arms of her chair and pushed herself up. She was a big woman, and since turning fifty, both standing up and sitting down had become more difficult. Her knees ached on the way up, her left hip ached when she walked, her knees, both hips and her lower back ached when she sat down. The doctor told her she needed to lose forty-five pounds, and had given her a brochure — *Weight Loss for Postmenopausal Women*. Betty had taken it seriously for a time, and had even joined a lunchtime weight-loss club sponsored by the Uganda Child Welfare Bureau. But she had no time for things like that now.

Betty creaked down the short hallway to Mr. Elijah Ngologoza's office. She could feel the humid air fusing to her skin, and would have liked to wash her face and hands at that very moment. But there was work to do.

Elijah Ngologoza smiled at Betty and moved a stack of files from the guest chair to the floor. He was lighter-skinned than Betty, a galaxy of freckles spotted his face and bald head.

"How is your Alfred, Betty Obote?"

"He is as comfortable as can be expected, thank you, Mr. Ngologoza." He was her third cousin, and even though they had known each other their entire lives, she felt uncomfortable talking to him about Alfred's condition.

"He's a good man, Betty Obote. You take good care of him; that's an order, you understand, woman?"

Betty smiled and nodded and handed the letter to Elijah Ngologoza.

"I don't know what to make of it, Mr. Ngologoza."

Betty watched Elijah Ngologoza scan the letter.

"Mildred Kamugasa says I should tell them that there are no refunds."

Elijah Ngologoza looked puzzled for a moment, then pushed his head back and laughed. It was a wonderful sound that echoed down the quiet hall, and Betty Obote laughed too.

"No refunds — that's beautiful! I must remember that. No refunds!"

"What do you want me to do, Mr. Ngologoza. I am really at a loss. I've tried to write a letter but I don't know where to start. I don't know what to say. These people, they are children sometimes."

Elijah Ngologoza nodded and brought his hand to his chin.

"They wear jeans to work, Mr. Ngologoza: *jeans*!"

Elijah Ngologoza tapped his hand on the desk. He folded and unfolded the letter. Betty Obote sat quietly, watching him reread it from the beginning. Occasionally, he frowned and shook his head. Finally, he lifted his eyes. "What we need to do, Betty Obote, is file this in the appropriate place." He smiled once again, then slowly crumpled the paper with one hand. He was laughing still as he flung the letter into the wastepaper basket, and his bubbling laughter continued as she pushed herself to her feet.

"Remember, Betty Obote," he called, as she made her way back down the hallway. "No refunds! That's official bureau policy now, Betty Obote; you pay your money and you take your chances!"

III. Methodology

Kyle was bivouacked in a fortress of blankets and pillows. He had cordoned off an area outside Nkunda's bedroom, and was on his back ready to deploy the vacuum.

Another pest-control guy had come and gone. He had been helpful in his way.

"This is very unusual. In North America we commonly see *Drosophila melanogaster* — vinegar flies." The pest-control guy had looked directly at Kyle as he spoke. He wore an orange jumpsuit with a large Capital Exterminators logo on the back — a cartoon wasp in handcuffs — and the name *Marcel* embroidered on a patch above his heart. Marcel was about Kyle's age, late twenties or early thirties, with very straight, sandy hair — Kyle had wiry hair and hated it — and gold-coloured, wire-rimmed glasses that made him seem quite serious. "Or members of the *Tephritidae* family: *Ceratitis capitata*, the medfly; *Anastrepha ludens,* or Mexican fruit fly — these are not uncommon. But this, I have never seen anything quite like it. Look —"

Marcel handed Kyle a Sherlock Holmes magnifying glass and, clamping a single fly with a pair of tweezers, held it up for Kyle to inspect. Kyle lifted the magnifying glass to his eye: light brown head and body, brown turtle-shell plates on its back, translucent wings freckled with black spots.

"My best guess: *Ceratitis cosyra*. The mango fruit fly. They are invasive, not native to North America. Usually hide out in produce: mango, papaya. Hence the name." Marcel took the magnifying glass from Kyle. "I will have to take it back to the office, do some research before I can give you a definitive ID."

Kyle nodded. "It's so strange to think there is a whole world of creatures around us that we never see."

"Scientists think there are something like 10 million *undiscovered* insect species in the world."

"No shit. It's like these alien creatures from outer space — fantastic creatures — all around us, but invisible."

"Sow bugs, carpet beetles, dust mites, book lice..."

"You just see something moving out of the corner of your eye, but never think to take a closer look."

"Exactly. That's exactly what I was thinking."

Later, after they had smoked a joint in the garage, Marcel told Kyle to drop his resumé off at head office. They were always hiring new guys, Marcel said: "I'll put in a good word for you, man." They bro-hugged at the doorway before Marcel left. Kyle watched the pest-control guy walk away, lilting slightly to the left to compensate for the weight of the tool box. And then Kyle remembered: the fruit flies.

He spent the rest of the morning patrolling the apartment. The flies had quickly come to associate the sound of the vacuum with death. Kyle wasn't sure how they did this. Perhaps they had a rudimentary communication system, releasing a certain chemical or flapping their wings at a particular speed, to signal danger. It made sense, evolutionarily speaking. Even tiny creatures needed a way to warn each other of danger.

Whatever the communication system, the defence strategy was ill-suited for Kyle's brand of attack. At the sound of the vacuum, the flies would take to the air and scatter, fleeing from whatever food source they were congregating around. But then they'd land and cower in the most obvious places: in the corners of the ceiling, in the cracks between the wall and the cupboard doors, on windows and mirrors. In flight, they actually had a chance: Kyle had to time it perfectly to catch them. But when he found them, lying low, they were doomed.

Kyle was still a little buzzed when Nikki came home from the Dr. Wasserman's office. She was carrying Nkunda in the detachable shell of the car seat her mother had given them for Christmas. His parents had been really supportive, and even paid the legal fees. But her parents had been against the adoption from the start, not only because they felt there were inherent difficulties when white parents adopted black babies — they weren't racist, just from a generation that seemed to care more about these sorts of things — but because they thought it was too soon. Nikki and Kyle had only been trying for a few years, and these things take time. They should relax, her parents said, stop worrying about having kids. Kyle would find another job, Nikki could cut down her hours at the bank and nature would take its course.

"You are still just lying there?"

"The pest-control guy just left."

"And?"

"He was cool."

"Cool, but what did he *say*?"

Kyle told Nikki about the mango fruit fly, and Nikki told Kyle about the doctor.

"Another prescription, something called albendazole."

"It sounds awful. What does it do?"

"Kills things. Like insect larvae. They use it on tape-worms. It's supposed to be good."

"Is it covered?"

"The pharmacist wasn't sure. I'm going to have to check my plan."

Nikki put the baby on the cushionless couch. Nkunda was sleeping with his head on an angle and a cookie in his hands. It looked very cute. Nikki took out her phone to take a picture. His birth name had been Joseph Kahwa, but she wanted something more traditional. They found Nkunda on an online baby-name site. Nkunda Joseph Kahwa-Kingstone. Had a nice ring to it. Maybe he would be a great man someday, a writer or politician.

"He can't take the medication with milk."

"Why not?"

"I don't know. But the pharmacist was very clear: no milk."

Nikki went to the kitchen counter to check the mail. She skimmed the small stack of bills and fast-food flyers.

Kyle called from the living room: "Pizza Planet has a two-for-one; just saying."

"Nothing from the agency?"

Kyle did not respond. Nikki stuck her head into the living room. Her husband had his headphones on now and was listening to some of that music she hated.

Nikki walked right up to him and put her hands over her ears. He pulled the headphones off and smiled: Nikki could hear the tinny guitars and drums.

"Nothing from the agency."

Kyle shrugged.

"You'd think they'd respond. You'd think they'd be concerned that something like this is going on."

Kyle shrugged again. "You'd think."

That night, Nikki searched the Internet while Kyle played with the baby. The computer screen was dotted with little flies; Nikki hypothesized that they liked the heat the screen gave off.

"Ewww, gawd." Nikki was looking at a picture of a milk-white ribbon, laid out in coils on a black table. "Says here that tapeworms can grow up to twelve feet long and live in a person for years without them ever knowing."

Kyle didn't say anything. He was once again on his back, now holding Nkunda in both hands, lifting him up as far as his arms could go, then quickly dropping his arms, pretending to let the baby fall. "Oh noooooo," he'd say in a silly high voice each time. Nkunda babbled and giggled, like a happy fountain.

"OMFG. There's a thing called a hookworm that gets into your intestines and feasts on your blood."

"I heard about a lady — *oh noooooo!* — who was bit in the head by a spider, and she got a big welt on her head and like five weeks later the welt burst open — *oh noooooo!* — and all these little spiders came crawling out."

"That's an urban myth, Kyle."

"Really? 'Cause I read it somewhere or saw it — *oh noooooo!* — on TV."

"I should google it."

"You should, baby. But I bet you a blowjob I'm right."

"Ha! You *wish*."

Later, they made love on the futon bed as Nkunda slept soundly in the crib next to them. Kyle whispered in Nikki's ear as he rubbed his naked body against hers, graphically describing a three-way with the two of them and Marcel, the pest-control guy.

"We should totally make this happen," he said, as he finally slid inside her.

"I so wanna be your slut. I so wanna make this happen for you."

They could hear Hector outside, meowing in the moonlight.

"Cat wants in," Kyle said, without missing a stroke. Nikki, ignoring the cat, spread her legs a little wider and dug her nails into her husband's shoulders.

"We should try earplugs," she said, just moments after she climaxed. Kyle was already almost asleep. "Earplugs would plug the little holes; they might really make a difference."

IV. Results

The bus ride home was longer than usual. A delivery truck had run into a tourist coach outside the Rubaga Cathedral; the street was blocked with pilgrims and loose chickens. When the thunderstorm came, the road flooded over and traffic had to be rerouted.

Betty Obote was further delayed when she stopped at the confectionary to buy poppy-seed cake. The girl in the bakery waved the flies away with one hand as she cut three slices for Betty.

"How is Mr. Obote, Madame?" The bakery girl handed Betty her treats in a greasy paper bag.

"He's doing well, Miss. Thank you for asking."

It was late when Betty Obote got home. Juliet, her daughter-in-law, was in the kitchen, preparing dinner: ugali, beans, fish. Betty placed her briefcase and bag of cakes on the counter and plugged the kettle in. She would have liked to sit and talk with her daughter-in-law, but Juliet had to rush off to start her shift at the hospital.

"He was good today, Mother," Juliet said, as she put a pink cardigan over her flowered dress. "Quiet, but he seemed to have a bit of an appetite."

Betty set aside a bowl of ugali and beans; fish did not agree with her. She took one of the cakes out of the bag and cut it in half, placing one half on a Wedgewood saucer — the dinner set had been a wedding gift from her father's uncle, a very wealthy Kampala importer. She set the other half aside, for later.

Arthur was in the living room, sitting in his armchair, a blanket cocooning him from the shoulders down. The TV was on but the sound was off; one football team was playing another.

"How are you today, old man?"

Alfred looked at her without turning his head. His eyes were moist and red, not from crying, Betty supposed — her Alfred did not cry — but from exhaustion.

"I bought some cakes for you. Shall I set them here?" She put the plate with half a slice of poppy-seed cake on the side beside a cup of water. Alfred half nodded, to thank her.

"There was an accident at the cathedral again. They should shut it down to coaches. It's always the coaches. They are pilgrims. Let them walk a little. A little walking will not kill them."

Alfred nodded again. They were lucky in their way. He had worked for almost thirty years at the Department of Agriculture; he had a pension with medical benefits.

Alfred reached out, his hand shaking, and for a moment Betty thought he was going to take the cake. But instead, he grasped the cup of water. He brought it very slowly to his lips, water splashing on his chin. Betty resisted the urge to help. He took a very long sip, his Adam's apple straining with each gulp.

The cancer was eating him from the inside. They had found the tumours early enough, the doctors thought, and removed the prostate. But Alfred had never seemed to fully recover from the operation. The nausea persisted, incontinence was a problem; he had neither the desire nor the ability to function sexually. Now it seemed his vital organs were wearing down, his liver and kidneys failing, his heart weakening; the last time the doctor came, he had to search for several minutes just to find a pulse.

"Such a day at the office. Mr. Ngologoza said he's going to give me a day off next week. I've been working too hard, he said. We'll say I'm working at home, he said. No one will know, he said."

Alfred was trying to set the cup back on the table. He was very focused on this simple task.

Betty had seen it before. When she worked at the AIDS clinic in Masaka years ago, it happened all the time. People would come, sickly but not sick, but once they found out they were positive, their bodies would turn on them.

"You haven't tried the cake, Alfred. You must try the cake."

Alfred shut his eyes and drew the blanket further up his neck. Betty tried to imagine what it was like for him.

Most of us go through life fearing death or pushing it out of our minds, like an inconvenient and unnecessary appointment. Alfred lived it, every moment. Death was inside him, outside him.

Soon Alfred had sunk into an uncomfortable sleep. His arms and legs moved fitfully; he seemed to gasp for every breath.

Betty pushed herself up from the chair, and while her knee did not hurt as much as it usually did, the pain was still there. She picked up the cup and plate and carried them to the kitchen. She put the half cake slice back in the bag and placed the dishes in the sink. She made a cup of tea and, looking at her beans and ugali, decided she no longer had an appetite for them. She fancied something sugary and went to the pantry to get a mango. It was plump and soft and Betty could imagine the taste of its sweet juice. But when she cut it open, there was the faint smell of rotting fruit, and instead of pulpy flesh, Betty found a generation of wriggling creatures, animated grains of rice.

She set the mango aside and went to the pantry to get another.

V. Discussion

Sometimes, on nights like these, when Nikki couldn't sleep, she imagined Uganda. In her mind, she thought of huts made of mud and straw, and pictured little pygmy men, in their *National Geographic* loincloths, carrying tiny wooden spears and blowguns, tracking antelope or water buffalo through the high, porridge-coloured grasses. She knew it wasn't like that, of course. Nkunda had been born

just outside Kampala, a city with a million and a half people or more, very modern, according to the guidebooks,
with high-rise hotels, shopping malls and Internet cafés.
She liked to imagine what life would have been like for
Nkunda had they not adopted him. Would he have grown
up in an orphanage, like the ones you see in those English
movies, with leering, preening, whiskered men and shrill
women who always seem to fundamentally hate the children in their care? She wondered what Nkunda's birth
mother and birth father had been like. Nkunda's eyes
were very distinctive — wide and asymmetrical. Did he
get them from his mother and father? Of course, Nikki
would never know the answer. No one knew who Nkunda's
father was; his mother, according to the records, died of
AIDS shortly after the child was born. Nikki wondered
what they would have been like, Nkunda's birth mother
and father. If they'd lived in America, had been Nikki and
Kyle's neighbours, say, would they have been friends?
And what of Nkunda himself? What opportunity would
there have been for him in Uganda? Would he have gone
to school? Or been sold at a young age to one of those
child labour companies, chained to a workbench to make
sports shoes or ladies' fashion accessories. The thought
of little Nkunda forced to work like that — of *any* child
forced to live in those conditions — made Nikki sad. She
had an urge to hold him.

Nikki lifted the blanket and slowly rolled out of bed.
Kyle had an early morning, and she didn't want to wake
him. He had a job interview at the pest-control place and
had been up late, studying.

*Fruit flies feed on decaying garbage like peelings and food
scraps.*

Nikki had quizzed him. He was very smart, when he applied himself.

Fruit fly larvae need standing water and organic waste material to survive.

By the time they'd gone to bed, he'd memorized facts about what the article on the pest-control website called the Top 10 Most Common Household Pests, everything from rats and woodlice to spiders and cockroaches.

Nikki got up slowly. Hector, who was sleeping at the foot of the bed, lifted his head slightly, yawned, then went back to sleep.

Nikki went to the crib and lifted the mosquito-net cover Kyle had bought from an online army surplus store — not so much to keep the flies from getting at Nkunda, but more to keep them contained so she and Kyle could get a good night's sleep.

A female fruit fly can lay up to five hundred eggs at a time.

She brushed a few flies from Nkunda's cheek. The earplugs seemed to be working. Nothing could get in or out. The medication too. Every day, there seemed to be fewer and fewer flies.

She leaned over, and as she lifted the baby from his crib, he let out a startled cry. Nikki drew him to her breast and lowered her head, singing lightly, *Hush, little baby, don't say a word…* Nkunda smiled, and snuggled against her. *Mama's gonna buy you a mockingbird.*

Nikki wanted to keep singing, but realized she didn't know any more of the words. She hummed instead, and as she did, she thought once again of the people at the Uganda Child Welfare League or whatever it was called, who didn't even care enough to respond to her letter. She was walking to the living room and, as she sat down on the couch, she thought of writing another letter to some international agency — there must be one — that monitored these sorts of things. She leaned back and put her feet up on the coffee table. She wanted to turn the TV on but she didn't want to wake Kyle. She wondered if they had cable TV in Uganda, and how many channels they got. She wondered if you could get KFC there and if they celebrated Christmas and, if so, if their Santa Claus was black. There were so many things she didn't know about Africa.

Nikki leaned forward and kissed her sleeping baby. She brushed one fruit fly from Nkunda's cheek and watched as another circled his ear, searching for a way inside. The fly buzzed around and around Nkunda's head, making a few aborted attempts to go in his ear, bumping into the sponge plug each time. Finally, the fly landed on the almost-white tip of Nkunda's ear. It walked around and climbed off and on the earplug. But there was no way in. Her baby was impenetrable, like a fortress, like a jungle.

Mose said, "Sleep, baby Jesus."

It was Christmas Eve, and there was a blizzard going on outside. Mose was sitting by the Christmas tree, playing with some Lego.

Diane was sitting on a couch, doing a Sudoku. She wasn't sure she heard him correctly.

"What did you say, hunny?"

He didn't answer right away, then said, "Sleep, baby Jesus."

"Why'd you say that, hunny?

But Mose didn't answer. A minute later, he tipped over. He was sound asleep.

Diane didn't like eggnog, so she was drinking a rum and

Sleep, Baby Jesus

Coke. She put her drink and Sudoku aside and went over and picked up Mose and took him to the boys' room. She lay him in his bed. Birdy was on the top bunk playing with some action figures.

"I'm gonna stay up to see Santa," he told his mom.

"That's nice, honey," she said, but knew he'd be asleep soon too. "You should put your jammies on."

She went back to the living room and took a sip of her rum and Coke. They were playing "Rocking Around the Christmas Tree" on the radio, but she wanted something more peaceful. She got up and fiddled with the dial till she found a station playing religious Christmas music.

Birdy called from the bedroom, "Are you gonna stay up and see Santa too, Mom?"

"I've already met Santa, so I'm fine."

A few minutes later, she went to check on Bird. He was down too. She didn't even bother putting on his jammies, she just tucked him in.

She went back to the living room and settled in again. She was good at Sudoku and had finished all the expert puzzles in one book and had started on another. She liked Sudoku because it made you think without really having to think. She liked how it was all about numbers but not really about numbers. You didn't have to add or subtract or divide, you just had to put the right number in the right spot. It's like they weren't really numbers at all, just objects with no meaning beyond their need to be put in the correct place.

Diane thought about going to bed, but she was enjoying the peace and quiet. She liked the carols on the radio.

She got up and went to the kitchen and poured herself another drink. It was a little stronger than she liked, but that was okay. She took a long sip and closed her eyes. She loved the taste of rum and Coke. It was spicy and made her feel warm inside. It was giving her a little buzz, and that was okay too. She liked to get a little buzz every now and then. The rum and Coke, the buzz — everything. It made her feel like Christmas.

"That's it then, Junior?"

"That's it, Daddy."

"This is goodbye?"

"This is goodbye."

"Leaving me here to —"

"You'll be perfectly fine."

"I should have killed you when I had the chance."

"Really, it's not that bad."

"I should have chopped you up and served you to your mother."

"Zounds, Daddy, we're not Romans."

"That would have served you both right."

"You'll get used to it here. The nurses are wonderful."

"I don't want to die."

"I know."

"This is the shits; it really is."

"Someone has to take care of you."

"I can take care of myself."

"Here's a riddle, Daddy: what walks on four legs, then two, then three?"

"Screw you."

"I'm going now."

"So go already."

Junior stops, then turns. "Hey, I can see Uranus."

"I never tire of that joke. Now, please do an old man a favour and fuck off."

"Goodbye, Daddy."

Slumped in the Arm- chair of the Gods©

"Goodbye, miserable fruit of my loins."
"I love you."
"You've got a wonderful way of showing it."

Junior was doing one-armed push-ups wearing nothing but black and yellow Lycra® swim briefs with the Odyssey Hotel wordmark, his official accommodation sponsor, emblazoned across the backside. Before suffering a serious bout of lateral epicondylitis — tennis elbow — Junior could do five hundred push-ups per arm. After an extensive rehab program, which included hydrocortisone therapy, steroid supplements, ultrasound and physiotherapy, Junior reached the point where he could comfortably complete 350 reps with his bad arm.

On the wall beside the Bowflex Xtreme® 2 SE Home Gym, in the rattan frame Missy had given him for his thirtieth birthday, Junior had a picture of Daddy accepting a gold medal from Navy Commander John Collins, father of the Ironman Triathlon. The medal reads: *Honorary Champion*. Collins presented it to Daddy after the 2003 Ironman Triathlon in Kona, Hawaii, where the old man finished with a time of 12:46:22, becoming in the process the oldest competitor (previous record holder: Walt Stack, who, at seventy-three, finished the Kono Klassic dead last and, at 26:20:00, set a record for slowest all-time Ironman finish). Beneath the photo is an alder end table with mother-of-pearl insets portraying two Greek wrestlers, their naked bodies entwined like lovers, each trying to dominate the other. On the table: an unopened, ten-pound container of Optimum Nutrition 100% Whey Gold Standard™ Double Rich Chocolate, a lactose-free, bio-available predigested protein — a great source of natural high-potency essential amino acids — and a bottle of Betaoxytol, a non-hormonal anabolic/anti-catabolic agent to help build lean muscle tissue, increase strength and performance, decrease body fat and enhance muscle recovery. Junior ran his hand across his bald head and remembered the little girl he'd met at the clinic, her own head bald from chemo, most of her jaw surgically removed: Persephone Beaumont. His work was dedicated to Persephone — to her and to the memory of his beloved late wife, Missy Hwan.

Junior slumped into the armchair, a classic-style Cub Chair reupholstered in vintage blue textured fabric, and opened a room-temperature Gatorade G Series Pro 01 Prime (delivering twice the sodium and three times the potassium of regular Gatorade, and with lots of B vitamins to help convert carbs to energy). The chair, he salvaged from Daddy's apartment. "I am a cancer survivor," he told the reporter from *Inside Triathalon* magazine. "Acute myelocytic leukemia with malignant granular leukocytes." The reporter nodded and made a note on her yellow notepad (AMPAD Gold Fibre® 20 lb. Watermarked Canary Ruled). Junior had a certain magnetism, which she found attractive. Plus, he was a cancer survivor. That brought out her maternal instinct.

Junior went to the closet and got his Asics Gel DX Trainer®s. "A classic," he told the reporter. "My cross-training choice for fifteen years." He put them on. He liked the feel of the shoe, stable and flexible like the DS Trainer®s of years gone by. He had a tendency to overpronate, a problem that the shoe's long second-density medial post consoled. Junior did his shoes up. *"Anima sana in corpore sano,"* he said, adjusting his shoelace. "A sound mind is a sound body." He stepped outside. He would run 10K before dinner. After dinner, he would swim 15K.

"Are you ready to roll?" he called to the reporter through the screen door.

She stood up. "Véronique," she said helpfully.

Véronique de Bernard followed him outside into the cool autumn air. They would jog slowly for five minutes. And then they would stretch.

Junior had a theory about cross-training.

"The Ironman needs a whole-body tune-up," he told the reporter from *Inside Triathlon*. "He, or she, needs to strengthen the heart, bones, muscles, and joints. It's not enough to enhance cardiovascular fitness, build muscle, reduce body fat, or enhance flexibility. The Ironman has to do it all."

Véronique raised the Olympus s832 Pearlcorder® microcassette recorder. Her pronator teres, already tender from an earlier fall, was hurting again, but she persevered. She didn't want to miss a thing.

"It's like that *Star Trek* episode from the original series, 'Who Mourns for Adonis' —"

"Episode 33, from the second season?"

"Exactly."

"The one where the giant hand —"

"Apollo's hand."

"— grabs the *Enterprise* as it approaches Pollux 4 in the Beta Geminorum system."

"Yes."

"I've always wondered — the title: there is no Adonis.

Très anachronique, n'est pas?" Véronique's breathing was noticeably laboured.

"It's an allusion, of course. *Peace, peace! he is not dead, he doth not sleep!* But, yes: anachronistic — should we slow down?"

"No. I'm fine."

"Because this is the part of the run where I usually speed up. But if you want, we can slow down. I can do some sprints later, before I go to bed."

Véronique tried to catch his eye, to see if this legendarily spotless god of fitness was flirting. Junior was looking a long way down the road, focused on his goal.

"But I interrupted: you were talking about cross-training."

"The point I was making is that there are Five Pillars of Fitness: aerobic conditioning, anaerobic conditioning, muscle strength, muscle endurance and flexibility. Ignore just one and all of them will fade *Star Trek-Apollo*-like. The Five Pillars need to be adored and worshipped, and that's why I don't cotton to arguments against cross-training."

Véronique already had a title in mind: "Who Mourns for the Ironmen?" Potential cover shot: Buddy Marks Jr. and his dad, Buddy Marks Sr., in full training gear and *Star Trek*© shirts. Maybe a Klingon in the background, if that was legal copyright-wise.

Junior continued. "Granted, if you have a narrowly defined goal — improving your time trials over one hundred metres, for example — then a targeted training approach might be effective, and certainly conventional wisdom would support you on that. But even there, for example, we've seen a dramatic decrease in world-record sprint times over the last decade, because, I think one could argue, track runners and their coaches have learned the value of cross-training. However, for the Ironman this is a moot point: as Kip puts it, our goal is general training excellence, and that means cross-training. We have no other option."

"Kip will be back, leading your ground team?"

"It wouldn't be an Ironman World Championship without Kip in my corner."

Véronique made a note: *Kip sidebar.* "I want to go in another direction..." She stalls for time as she flips the Panasonic® RT 904MC ninety-minute microcassette and raises the Olympus® s832 again. "You're widely regarded as one of the most consistent competitors in Ironman history, coming fourth in overall points for Ironman of the Year six out of the last eight years. Yet you've never placed first in a sanctioned event. So, two questions: how do you account for your remarkable consistency, and what's holding you back from taking that elusive gold medal?"

"I'll answer the second question first, and it really begs another question — why did I get into Ironman in the first place? Of course, Daddy's influence was important —"

"Of course."

"— but for me the sport has always held a spiritual element. Winning a competition, in and of itself, has never been important to me. Athletic participation, mental focus, the pursuit of personal excellence, physical pain — when pushed to the extreme — have a potent, transcendent effect."

"While your father is notorious for his finish-at-all-costs mentality."

"True. But he comes from a different epoch. When

Daddy started, guys would smoke a couple cigarettes, eat a steak, then swim two and a half miles. They'd stop for waffles halfway through the bike stage. You couldn't get them to drink a glass of water, afraid it would give them stitches. You didn't have science then, so you had to rely on bravado and ritualized superstitions."

"And question one?"

"How I account for my remarkable consistency?"

"Yes."

"Well, again, that's hard to put in a simple sentence. Certainly Persephone Beaumont and her relentless courage and optimism have been an inspiration. And Missy..."

Véronique instinctively dropped her eyes at the mention of Junior's late wife. "You must miss her terribly."

Junior nodded, his eyes welling up. He composed himself. "But if I had to point to just one thing, I would again credit my dad."

"Your dad? Like, you're running for him?"

"More like running *from* him. Every race, I imagine Daddy is right behind me, trying to catch me. And that spurs me on. Fear of Daddy. That's the secret of my consistency."

"One last question for our readers, Junior: how do you like your father's chances in the Kona Klassic this year?"

"Well, if he's there — and that's a big if — but if he's there, I'm going to annihilate him. I'll eat him for breakfast and spit him out in partially chewed morsels for the rats and the dogs to feast on."

"It's a race to the death?"

"Exactly as billed: the Run for Our Lives."

"What we have here is a basic inability to communicate."

"I disagree, Daddy."

"How so?"

"I think what we have here is a basic ability to overcommunicate."

"The difference being?"

"The difference being that not only do we not not-understand one another, but we understand one another too well. Every nuance, every visual cue, every shade of meaning is completely comprehensible. We are communicating too much all the time. That's as big a problem as not communicating at all. It's the difference, say, between a drought and a flood, both profound in their effect, but with contradictory — some might say opposite — root causes and distinct solutions. In our case, the flood, more water will only make things worse."

"I love you, Junior."

"I know, Daddy."

"But I'm going to beat you."

"So, you're really going to do it? Come out of retirement? Leave the milky comforts of the Shady Rest Hotel?"

"You bet, Junior. I'm not done yet. First I'm going to whip your butt in the Ironman."

"Yes?"

"And then I'm going to kill you."

"Not unless I kill you first, Daddy."

"Is that a challenge?"

"It's whatever you want it to be."

"Right. May the best man win, Junior."

"No: may the least worst man not lose."

Buddy Marks Sr. A mythological figure in the Ironman pantheon. He was in Oahu at the Perimeter Relay when

John Collins first starting talking about Eddy Merckx's 96 vo_2 max level (put in perspective, a full-grown male cheetah in peak condition has a vo_2 of 116) and kicking around the idea of a competition to determine which athletes were the fittest: cyclists, runners or swimmers. And while he wasn't there at the Waikiki Swim Club when Collins first proposed the idea of combining the Roughwater Swim (2.4 miles), Around-Oahu Bike Race (115 miles) and Honolulu Marathon (26.219 miles) into a single event, Buddy Sr. was on deck at the first Kona Klassic — it was his guys that gave John Dunbar beer when he ran out of water in the marathon leg, knocking Dunny out of the running for top spot but giving him a great story to tell, and while Buddy Sr. was well off Gordie Haller's 11-hour, 46-minute, 58-second pace, he completed the race, something not everyone who started that day could say. And it was there, keeled over just past the finish line, that Buddy Marks Sr., still panting, uttered the phrase that would become his (literal) trademark: *Last one there's a bitch!*™

Even then, Buddy Sr. was the oldest competitor, and in every subsequent Klassic, sixteen straight years, he was in the top one or two, age-wise, yet never finished out of the first thirty. When all was said and done, he had five Top 15 finishes and won the Senior Men's Division a record seven times.

Myths abound. It's said he developed stamina as a kid, running numbers for Frank "Mr. Big" Balistrieri, legendary Milwaukee Mafia crime boss. And while he would neither confirm nor deny the stories, let the records show that he did do time in the Minard E. Hulse Juvenile Detention Center, in Vernon Hills, Illinois, for truancy and incorrigible behaviour, and a few years later, following a dishonourable discharge for getting drunk and deserting his post at the Presidio of Monterey army base, a six-month stint at Alcatraz, where he became only the second man in history to successfully escape from the Rock. He made the treacherous swim to Fisherman's Wharf in less than thirty-five minutes, then waited patiently on a bench to be recaptured. "What took you guys so long?" he said when the cops finally caught up with him. "I'm freezing my ass off here." The warden was so impressed with the feat that he personally knocked two months off Buddy Sr.'s sentence.

Best known for his athletic achievements, Buddy Sr.'s prowess in the boudoir and the barroom is almost as legendary. He was married five times, twice to Miss America Pageant finalists, and sired seven children, the youngest of whom, Buddy Jr., was born when Buddy Sr. was well into his fifties. And what can you say about his capacity for the bottle? At sixty, he was selected — along with former world heavyweight boxing champion Rocky Marciano (49-49-43, with a sixty-seven-inch reach) — as the face of the seminal Johnnie Walker "When Two Fists Aren't Enough" ad campaign.

At seventy, and much to the chagrin of his fellow Milwaukeeans, Buddy signed an exclusive sponsorship deal with Guinness (worldwide beer sales in excess of 1.8 billion imperial gallons per annum, a wholly owned subsidiary of the Diageo alcoholic beverage consortium), which required him, among other things, to drink a minimum of six cans of stout during the marathon leg of every triathlon he competed in. At eighty, he was fired by Wieden+Kennedy, Nike's agency of record, for showing up drunk to a kids' charity run in Palo Alto. Nike rehired him two weeks later, bowing to pressure from the international running community. Within days, a photo appeared on Facebook pages around the world: Buddy Marks Sr., standing at the finish line with a comely blonde fifty years his junior, guzzling a cold Guinness, a photoshopped priapic bulge in his running shorts, and at the bottom, a giant Nike swoosh and the caption *Just do her!* And that's how the Buddy Marks meme was born.

Buddy remains a fixture in his native Milwaukee. It's said that residents of the Milwaukee–Racine–Waukesha Metropolitan Area (the thirty-ninth most populous region in the United States) set their watches based on Buddy Marks Sr. sightings, so regular is his training routine. And last year, for his ninetieth birthday, the mayor presented Buddy with a key to the city at a gala celebration. Thousands of Milwaukeeans came out to stand in the shadow of the teutonic city hall's clock tower (at 350 feet, the tallest building in the city until finally surpassed, in 1970, by the unconsciously ironic Late International–style Firstar Bank building) to have a slice from the giant birthday cake (the second-largest public cake in Milwaukee history, incorporating 1,200 half-sheet slabs and 2,000 pounds of icing) and watch the guest of honour dance a drunken jig atop a giant Pabst Blue Ribbon® can.

Lately, Junior had been focusing on his core.

"Most muscles are dynamic, and move you forward in some way, if we are using *forward* in its most dynamic sense." Junior was speaking to the graduating class of the Abraham Lincoln High School in San Francisco, as part of the San Francisco Unified School District's Lead the Leaders Inspirational Speakers Series. He was wearing an Adidas® Supernova Gore Jacket, black with silver trim and silver bolts on the sleeves, over a black Adidas® Sequencials EQTIO Graphic Short Sleeve T, and a pair of black 3-Stripes Wind Pants (again, Adidas®, his official non-competition clothing supplier). "Core muscles — your abs, hips and lower back — are reactive. They are the first muscles to respond before any other muscle moves. They anticipate, analyze and act without conscious intervention. They are called 'core' because they are fundamental to everything we do."

Junior was a big believer in core exercises — Plank, Push-up Plank, V-sit Hold, Twisting Crunch, Lying Glute Push-up, Superman with a Twist — and that the beauty of the core lay in its simplicity. One didn't need a lot of expensive equipment or even a gym membership to work the core. He ran the class through an exercise he had learned, he told them, from his trainer and spiritual advisor, four-time Olympic™ medalist Kipchoge "Kip" Keino. Junior told the kids to sit up tall, with both feet planted firmly on the floor. Next, he instructed them to consciously tighten their abdominal muscles, "like," he said, "you are really trying to hold in a big fart coming from deep in the pit of your stomach." Then he told the kids to squeeze their shoulders together and hold themselves upright, raising one foot at a time, slowly, surely. At the same time, he told the students to curl forward, leading with the shoulders. Hold for a second. Then return your foot to the floor.

Junior got the kids to repeat the exercise, lifting the other foot. And then counted off twenty reps — one foot, then the other — ten times each.

"Congratulations, ladies and gentlemen, you've just

worked your core. It didn't cost you anything, except thirty seconds of your time. You didn't even have to get off your butts."

Junior waited for the laughter to subside before switching slides: a mostly black-and-white shot, the amaranth-pink headband in nine-year-old Persephone Beaumont's hair the only show of colour, drawing attention to the little girl's bright and expressive eyes and away from her surgically deformed lower jaw.

"But you're not just learning a way to get tight abs, guys. I'm talking about the core. I'm talking about the fundamental stuff that keeps us together, keeps us human. I am talking about the core that lies behind my success as a cancer survivor; I am talking about the core that informs Persephone's Army® and has made it the fasting-growing service organization in North America today, for young people between the ages of fifteen and twenty-three. I'm talking about your past, your present, your future. I'm talking about Persephone's Army®, and your place in it..."

"Mr. Marks —"

"Call me 'Junior.'"

"Ah...Junior." Nervous laughter. "Can you comment on the Kona Klassic? Is it really a Race to the Death, as the Facebook and Twitter feeds are saying? Or is that just a bunch of, you know, hype?"

"I'm not here to talk about the Klassic, son. This is really Persephone's day. But I will say one thing; have you seen the movie *Dead Man Walking*? Well, get ready for the sequel: *Dead Ironman Running*."

"How would you like to die, Junior?"

"In my sleep, Daddy, two weeks after my one hundredth birthday."

"You're being very optimistic."

"Optimism's in my genes, Daddy. You know that."

"And your second choice?"

"I don't know. I've already survived one death, watched life leak out of me, helium-from-balloon-esque. Something quick and painless next time, I suppose. Like a bullet to the head."

"Or a knife to the heart, Junior?"

"Or a knife to the heart. And you, Daddy? How would you like to die?"

"Naked, in bed with two women, moments after getting off, killed by a massive heart attack, two weeks after your one hundredth birthday."

"And I'm the optimistic one?"

"I'm not optimistic, just ambitious."

"Barring that, how would you like to die, Daddy?"

"From joy, having just crossed the finish line, Junior, just ahead of you."

I think it's remarkable that every time you look into the night sky, you are looking directly into the past." Junior was standing on the warm sand of Dig Me Beach on Kailua Bay. It was still early, not even 5 AM, and he was eating a whole-grain bagel topped with a thin layer of almond butter. Carbs, protein; nothing too heavy. "Polaris is 430 light years away. The flickering we see today was generated before Shakespeare wrote his first play, before Galileo had turned his telescope to the stars, before the first recorded European colonies were set up in North America…"

Véronique had placed the Olympus Pearlcorder on the

rock wall beside Junior and was crouched on the ground next to him, framing a shot with her Panasonic Lumix® GF3 (12.1 megapixel, 17.3 x 13.0 mm Live MOS). It was a great POV, looking up at Junior as he gazed off into the galaxy.

"*Inside Triathlon* readers want to know, Junior: are you nervous?"

Junior tilted his head and looked down at her. Very boyish. If she slid a couple paces to the left, she could get the Applebee's SacroPro™ 2000 sacrificial altar in the background. Perfect. She snapped a couple more pics.

"I don't get nervous. Nervous is for people who need to win or who are striving for some kind of personal-best time. That's not who I am. I'm not worried about the other guy; I am not worried about the clock; I am not worried about potentially, you know, slipping from this mortal coil. I am racing for the past, for the memory of Missy, and for the future, for Persephone and all the countless Persephones in the world. If I am racing against anyone, it's me."

"There's a lot at stake this time."

"There always is."

Junior stood. He was dressed simply, a De Soto® Men's Forza® Bib Tri Short and cotton T with the Persephone's Army® wordmark over the breast. Junior didn't wear any sponsored gear in competition. It was one of his rules. He liked to keep things pure, to run for the sake of running, to run to honour Persephone.

Junior turned slightly and bent over, stretching his lower back and hamstrings, and for a moment Véronique let down her professional guard. He had a beautiful body

— smooth, perfect lats and pecs, defined ab ridges and a firm line running along the bottom of the torso, massive articulated glutes and quads that rippled through the thin covering. She imagined slipping down the shoulder straps of the bib and peeling off the Forza® compressor fabric, rubbing her hands along Junior's perfectly formed and semi-celibate contours.

"Is it true . . . "

"Yes?"

"Is it true that you never . . . engage in sexual activity for one month directly preceding and directly following a sanctioned event?"

"Is that what you really want to ask me?"

Véronique shook her head: no. "You still think of her all the time, don't you?"

"Missy?"

"Yes, I can see it in your eyes. There's a kind of pain there, a kind of — *je ne sais quoi* — *defeat?*"

Junior straightened his body, lifting his hands above his head, clasping them together as he raised one leg and brought his foot level to his groin — a perfect yoga tree. Véronique took another picture. Her breath shallow, her cheeks flushed, she watched him close his eyes and focus.

"Tell me again about that episode, Junior? Tell me what happened to the gods?"

"Apollo and his fellow gods were intergalactic travellers who made earth their home for a time. Once, they had been venerated and worshipped by humans, but in time, as wonder gave way to logic, myth to science, the humans turned their backs on the gods. They let the temples go fallow. They stopped making sacrifices. They forgot how the stories began and ended. Soon, some of the lesser gods — Zephyrus, god of the west wind; Ceto, goddess of ocean dangers; Enyalius, a minor god of war — were passing from memory, until eventually all of the gods were either forgotten or, at best, distant memories. So the gods went back to their home planet, Pollux IV, but with no one there to worship them, no to believe in them, they began to fade into the wind. One by one they dissolved — not dead, as we humans understand it, but awakened from the dream of life, so to speak, becoming in their diminishment something greater."

The organizers had given them special dispensation: their own start time, smack between the professional women at six-thirty-five and the amateur age groupers at seven o'clock. This was to accommodate the TV commitments as much as anything. An estimated 75 million people would be watching the wet start live, with another 100 to 150 million expected to tune in later on tape delay. The producers had paid their money and didn't want to run the risk of losing Daddy and Junior in the chaos of those open minutes in the water.

Dig Me Beach and the Kailua-Kona pier were packed. People were literally clinging to rocks, just to get a view, just to say they were there at the start of the historic Run for Our Lives. The medics were kept busy. A women from Ecuador broke two ribs and suffered a mild concussion falling from the top of one of the thirty-eight temporary grandstands organizers had set up along the one-and-a-quarter-mile stretch of shore that followed the opening leg. Another woman, an Asian diplomat, passed out in the early-morning heat; she had a miscarriage in the ambulance on the way to the Kona Community Hospital. Persephone was there too, right in front, on the pier beside the Applebee's SacroPro™ 2000 sacrificial altar, in her custom Soaring Eagle® T-Frame v-Cage Racing Chair, a lei of fresh pikake circling her neck, discreetly shielding her jaw.

Junior's strategy was simple. He wasn't about to let the simplicity of The Swim fool him. On paper, it was a single, counter-clockwise loop, there and back. In practice, you fought swells and chops and tidal currents that pulled you the entire way out, but pushed against you the whole way back. Endurance, patience, adaptability: those were critical to success in The Swim. Daddy was a fish, and even at his advanced age he was hands-down the better swimmer. Junior would follow, literally, in Daddy's wake, let the old man set the pace and wear himself down. Junior could afford to fall a little behind on The Swim; it was only 2.4 miles, and there was plenty of opportunity in the subsequent 112 miles of intense cycling to make up for lost time.

Daddy tried to stare Junior down as they waded into the bathtub-tepid water of Kailua Bay. Buddy Sr. stood for a moment, letting the water soak into his retro Nike ball-hugger racing shorts and finishing the last puffs of an El Rey del Mundo Coronas de Luxe (ring gauge: 42; length: 5.5 in.). He flicked the butt into the sea water. Junior pushed it aside with one hand and crouched, waiting for the starter pistol.

Things got off pretty much as planned. Buddy Sr. liked a fast start and took off at full speed. He preferred the Australian crawl, and despite two shoulder replacements in his mid-eighties, still pulled it off beautifully. True, his stroke was a little unstudied, choppy even, but he had a marvellous range of motion, and slid through the water with a hypnotic rhythm that never seemed to vary. Junior favoured the breaststroke — always had — admittedly, the slowest stroke sanctioned by FINA, the International Swimming Federation, but also the most ancient stroke and most difficult to master. Connoisseurs agreed: Junior's execution was flawless.

Daddy was still in sight when his son made the halfway point, an exaggerated spike around an anchored sailboat, and Junior was feeling comfortable with his progress despite the current's drag, until he felt a sudden, agonizing pang in his left calf. He hoped it was only a tweak of some kind and slowed for a moment. The pain subsided, but came back seconds later with an even greater intensity. Cramp.

Junior let his leg go slack. Cramps and stitches had been a problem since the cancer first struck; the disease and subsequent treatment had compromised his blood's ability to store and distribute oxygen. One of the advantages of the breaststroke was that the loss of his leg power was disruptive but not catastrophic. He persevered, watching his father pull further ahead until he was lost in the rolling chop of Kailua Bay.

Kip was on the radio when Junior reached the shore: Daddy had a good eight minutes' lead. Junior ran to his bike, stopping at the foot of the sacrificial altar to give Persephone Beaumont a quick hug. She held on to his hand as he tried to pull away. "I believe in you," she said, her voice never able to rise above a whisper. He kissed her forehead and pushed himself away. Now the seconds were beginning to matter.

The sun was already out in full as Junior hit the bike; the temperature was climbing into the eighties. It was going to be a scorcher.

Junior's ride was a Felt DA4, an update on a durable classic, with the same Nano carbon frame as the DA1, an advanced MMC carbon chassis, TTR3 alloy aero wheels (the super-narrow front hub flanges got you up and running) and FSA/Vision Metron shifters, made for seamless gearing; you could almost feel the BB30 time-trial chainset think as it churned around the Shimano Dura Ace gears.

As for Buddy Sr, he changed bikes like they were shoes. Last year, he was on a customized BMC Timemachine TM01 SRAM Red. The year before that, a somewhat disastrous ride on a Cervélo P2. This time out, he turned to a Specialized Shiv Pro to try and gain an aerodynamic advantage (control on the decline had always been an issue for him). Not the lightest bike on the road, but made to fuck with the mountains and killer crosswinds. The FACT carbon-armed, oversized axle cranks, the wider-than-normal 52/36-tooth chainring and 11-28T cassette, the SRAM Red mechs, shifters and KMC chain — everything was designed for power and control.

When it came to the cycles, you could call it a draw. Besides, the choice of bike was really an illusion. Reality consisted of bucking trade winds that could gust in excess of forty miles an hour (Junior had seen full-grown men blown right off the road), mountain grids that ranged anywhere from five to eighteen per cent and strangulating humidity that could make 85 degrees feel like 105.

It wasn't enough to be in shape for The Bike. You had to be *ready*. The Bike was one mountain after another, relentless, the ups requiring power, conditioning and torque, the downs pushing a rider's driving skills to the limit.

Junior started well. He managed to catch a small tail-wind on the Hot Corner at Makala Boulevard — Buddy Sr. had been stuck in a crosswind — that kick-started his ride. By the time he cross-sectioned the city — spotting now and then Buddy Sr.'s strategically discarded Guinness cans and Subway wrappers — and made his way out to the Queen Ka'ahumanu and her lava fields, he picked up almost a minute on Buddy Sr.'s time. But he also started running into other riders, some of the slower female pros and even some of the men, who'd had equipment or other problems and were riding now for pride.

The other riders were creating problems. Junior was getting boxed in on the corners, and those little gullies between the rocky peaks were treacherous as inexperienced cyclists, unfamiliar with nuances of Queen K's thermals, braked and weaved without warning. By the time he reached Waikoloa, he had lost all the time he had gained.

Junior persevered. He managed to shake most of the traffic through the constant ascent into Hiwa, and by the turnaround he was feeling comfortable and on his game. He had a nervous feeling as he was passing the lone bike he had encountered on the descent. The rider, a leathery and vaguely Eastern European–looking woman on an older model Argon 18 Gallium Pro, was struggling to open a GU™ Jet Blackberry energy gel pack (a one-hundred-calorie hit of maltodextrin for energy, sodium and potassium to replenish electrolytes, plus "a unique blend of amino acids to combat muscle fatigue, accelerate the conversion of carbohydrates into usable energy and help maintain mental focus") with her teeth, and looked up at Junior for a moment, her eyes widening as she realized she was being passed by one of the greatest living triathletes, and at almost the same instant, letting out a little cry as a crosswind caught her. She sideswiped Junior, then slid under him. He rode overtop her leg and front tire before his own front wheel got locked in her handles. He did a complete half flip and found himself seconds later on his back in the middle of the 920, looking up into the clear Hawaiian sky.

Junior lay there for a minute or two, the wind knocked out of him, his left elbow in pain, taking stock of his injuries and listening to the other rider, blood flowing from a cut just above her eye, saying *Gott im Himmel* over and over again.

The damage to his Felt DA4 was minimal. A couple loose spokes. A flat. A chip on the handles. Some quick repairs and, despite a goose-egg welt on his elbow, he was ready to roll again.

"Run your race," Kip cautioned over the radio as Junior climbed back on his ride. "Don't fight the clock and don't chase him. Resist the urge to catch your father. Ignore the illusions."

By the time he made it back to Kailua, Junior's elbow was throbbing and he was a full nineteen minutes behind the old man. He hadn't pushed it though. His mantra now was "pace." There was still an entire marathon left to run: focus was everything.

Junior slipped out of his Spiuk SEC-SEG Triathlon® cycling shoes and into a pair of freshly broken-in Asics Gel DS Trainer®s. He liked to take The Run relatively easy at the start. Right off the bat, there was a slight incline up Palani Road, and a lot of runners liked to push it and pick up time while the running was still easy, but Junior kept it in low gear. He wanted to replenish his fluids and electrolytes; he needed to transition from his bike legs to his road legs.

He'd caught up to the middle of the Ladies Pro group and there were dozens of Men's Pro stragglers on the road. Junior pushed himself into the middle of the pack, letting the people ahead of him create some drag, while the rest of the group acted as a buffer from the wind and humidity. By the time they took the sharp right on Kuakini Highway, Junior was ensconced in a passel of runners. Even though every spectator crowding the sidewalks was trying to catch a glimpse of him, Junior slipped through the city leg of The Run largely unnoticed.

Theoretically, he had the edge in The Run. Daddy was a plodder; give him a steady pace and he could run forever. Thing is, you didn't need to run forever. You needed to run 26.2 miles, to match the Pheidippides's feat, but not an inch further. Daddy understood machismo, he understood showmanship, but he lacked the particular kind of discipline one needed to slow down when the situation warranted.

The signs were everywhere. Daddy had gone through a dozen Guinness Stout — Junior had kept track since the start of The Ride — and when Junior reached the five-mile turnaround point by the stone church on Ali'i Drive, he saw a telltale can of Rockst*r® Recovery Grape at the side of the road. It wasn't just a nod to Daddy's official energy-drink sponsor, it was a silent message that he was caffeinating up: Daddy was going for it.

There was a downside, of course. Caffeine had a dehydrating effect, something Daddy, because of his advanced age, should have been wary of. More than anything, at ninety-plus years and a hundred-plus degrees on the humidex, dehydration was Daddy's greatest enemy. But you can't unteach an old dog even older tricks. Daddy was marking his territory; a discarded Rockst*r® Recovery can precisely every mile.

By the time he reached the Kuakini Highway, Junior had found his pace while staying comfortably in his zone 3 heart rate. He was being passed often at this point, mostly by wiry fiftyish men and women who'd caught their second wind and were letting the easy flats and gently rolling hills seduce them. He would no doubt be passing these runners himself soon enough, discarded Daddy-drink-can-like on the highway's shoulder, bent over gasping for breath or on their backs shaking from dehydration and kidney overload. *Run your race. Resist the urge to catch your father.*

The pain in his calf was building again, although he'd loaded up on potassium and kept himself hydrated to keep the cramping at bay, and while he'd tightly bandaged his elbow in the transition tent on Kailua Pier, Junior had to be careful to avoid sudden arm movements. But that's what the Ironman taught you. More than anything, you had to ignore the pain. Swim through it, ride through it, run through it — no matter who you were or where you went or what you did, the pain would be there. You had to work with it, not rise above it or block it from your mind or separate yourself from it, but link yourself to it, make an atomic, chemical bond, you/pain, and let it redefine and define you.

By the time Junior reached the ten-mile point, back on

the Queen K Highway, he had started to gain some ground. Kip had radioed: Daddy had just entered the Energy Lab, the long stretch of lava fields at the sixteen-mile mark. The site of a solar-and-sea-water-powered industrial park and alternative energy research facility, the Energy Lab section of The Run was hot — blacktop temperatures regularly approached 120 degrees — and flat and hit you just at the point when the marathon went from being mostly physical to entirely mental. This is where you saw even the best triathletes crumble, collapsing, their minds broken, or reduced to shuffling parodies of themselves-as-runners. It was the point in the triathlon where the greatest losses occurred, but also, for some, the greatest gains.

Six-plus miles. That was a lot of ground to make up in a foot race. But Junior had found his pace. He wasn't pushing yet; he knew there would be a time for that. But he had a rhythm going, almost tribal: *Miss-eeee, Persephoneeee. Miss-eeee, Persephoneeee. Miss-eeee, Persephoneeeee...*

He was encouraged, having reached the Energy Lab turnoff without crossing paths with Daddy. That meant more gains. Although he wished his father no ill, he really did, he knew this was the make-or-break point for Daddy.

The mind games continued. Rockst*r®Recovery cans were marking every quarter mile now, an almost superhuman level of caffeine and sugar; the wrappers — Snickers®, PowerBar® Pure & Simple Energy Roasted Peanut Butter energy bar, Cheetos® Crunchy Flamin' Hot® Limón Cheese Flavored Snacks — telling Junior that not only was Daddy carbing up, but at the same time laughing in the face of science. Then, three quarters of a mile in, there he was. At first, as the heat waves rose from the blacktop, Junior couldn't quite grasp what he was looking at. It may have been some kind of animal or machine, writhing or pumping or otherwise moving. But as he got closer, it was clear that this figure was, at the very least, humanoid. With every step, the image became clearer: Daddy, in perfect lines and planes, performing one-armed push-ups, changing arms every stroke with a studied hand-to-hand hop.

"One thousand and six, one thousand and seven, one thousand and eight..." he counted out loud, in an effortless and perfectly modulated voice, as Junior plodded past.

That was the moment he almost lost it, the moment Junior almost gave in to temptation. *I could book it*, he thought. *I could catch the old man now, pass just as the arrogant bastard hits the Queen K...* And for a moment he somehow thought this would end the pain, not just of the race, but of a lifetime of small defeats and inconstancies.

But then he thought of Missy's face, and how they'd never recovered the body after the accident, and of the last words she had ever said to him, just before she'd left for work: "You never take me running in the morning."

Junior dropped his head and slowed his pace.

He felt strangely at peace as he finished the Energy Lab leg. His calf muscle throbbed, his elbow was numb with pain. But he'd hit his pace again — *Miss-eee, Persephoneeee. Miss-eeee* — and when he reached the Queen K turnoff, the six-mile home stretch, he was ready to race. Now was the time to accept the pain, to draw on it and on all the energy and mental reserves he had left.

"The bear is in the meadow, you copy? Roger."

"Copy that, Kip. What's his status? Roger."

"He's definitely hit the wall. He's carbon-loading and hydrating like crazy. Might be too much too late. Roger."

"K. Roger."

"Where you at, Junior? Roger."

"I'm on the home stretch, baby. Feeling good. Roger."

"Okay. You're about three miles back. It's def possible. Run your race, Junior, run your race. Roger."

"Copy that. Roger. Over and out."

There's a melodic quality to The Run. A music that no one can hear except the runner. Not every runner hears it, and no two runners hear exactly the same tune. It's indescribable, really. Missy once said it was like the most profound silence locked in the middle of a symphony so beautiful it could never be written, and if ever written, never performed. You don't hear it at the beginning, of course, or in the middle, and you don't hear it if you listen for it. It's like sleep, or that immeasurable moment between being asleep and being awake. That's when the music comes. When everything else is gone: hope, pain, love, promise, loss, consciousness — nothing. Then, a music that can't exactly be heard, only imagined in the most animal places of the brain. It's at this point that you leave yourself. You are no longer the runner, you have become an object as significant and insignificant as the other objects around you. And then, if you're lucky, you understand that the end is nearly in sight. For Junior, this usually happened around the twenty-four-mile mark, as he realized that the race was almost done. There was always a momentary pang of soul-breaking disappointment, the it-is-finished flash when you realize that this Thing, this Race, that has consumed your every waking thought for months, has now been almost completely consumed by you. Then, as Junior can attest, the adrenaline takes over.

Known for his consistency over the long haul, Junior also had one of the most legendary kicks in triathlon history. He knew just when to turn on the afterburners, somehow calculating the exact amount of energy and reserves he had left to finish a race. He'd already started his sprint as the Palini Road turnoff — which would take him back for one more circuit of the Kailua-Kona proper — rolled into view. And then he saw, in the distance, the familiar outline. Daddy was persevering, but just barely. He had a certain unsteady cadence, evident even though he still had a good quarter-mile lead on his son.

Once again, Junior had to resist the urge to give chase. He tried to visualize the remaining route, down Palani Road, right at the Hot Corner onto the Kuakini Highway to begin a final loop of the town, down to Hualalai Road, right onto Hualalai and following it to Ali'i Drive. There, the finish line awaited.

By Kuakini, Daddy was in his sights. Junior could hear his belches, smell his farts; he could almost taste the acid and bile rising in the back of Daddy's throat.

Midway down Hualalai, he had almost caught up. He slowed and slid in behind Daddy, allowing the old man to set the pace. It was almost too painful for Junior to take. He could hear his father's every laboured breath, count the seconds between each uneven step. His hands shaking, he was trying to tear open another PowerBar® wrapper. Junior backed off a step.

"You think I can't hear you? You think I don't know you're there." Daddy seemed to need to gulp to finish each sentence. "You think I haven't thought this through, boy? You think I haven't saved anything up in the tank? Then just pass me, boy. See what happens. Try and pass me!"

Junior remained silent, then smiled. "I can see Uranus."

"Shut up, Junior. Just shut the fuck up."

They were in front of the Hulihe'e Palace when Junior made his move. He first tried to pass Daddy on the right, but the old man veered over and impeded his path. So Junior did a quick fake, speeding as if to take him outside on the left, then cutting back to pass Daddy on the right side. The old man seemed to growl as Junior passed, and tried to grab the edge of Junior's bib with shaking fingers.

Junior kept his speed up for a few moments, then settled back down into his pace. But as the crowd behind him roared, he turned to see Daddy, his face red, his eyes almost empty of life, in full stride.

From there on, it was back and forth, Daddy using his height and longer stride, his pure animal intensity, to inch ahead; Junior, focused now only on the finish line, pushing himself to go faster.

Junior could now count the strides to the pier entrance and finish line, and just as he was about to give his final kick, he heard his father's anguished cry — *anguished* was the only word to describe it. The crowd immediately hushed. Junior turned to see Daddy sprawled face down on the road. His legs and arms twitching, his nose to the pavement, a yellowy froth bubbling from bloodied lips.

151 •

Junior slowed for a moment, thought about stopping. It was completely conceivable that Daddy was faking.

Junior took a few more steps toward the finish line, then turned back. "Medic!" he called. "Daddy's down, we need a medic!"

As he rushed to his father's side, the old man's breathing had grown more laboured. Junior gently turned Daddy onto his back. Daddy's eyes rolled back and he seemed to be saying something. Junior leaned closer and listened, but although he could see Daddy's lips move, he could only hear deep, laboured breathing. Daddy reached up and grabbed Junior by the bib. "Last one there's a bitch™," Daddy said through the delirium. "Last one there's a total fucking bitch."

The photo is now iconic. Junior, his elbow in a makeshift bandage, his legs buckling under the weight, carrying his unconscious father over the finish line like some kind of broken parody of the *Madonna and Child*. They are surrounded by dozens of officials and supporters, many of them in tears, each one holding their arms out, ready to support Junior should he falter. Persephone Beaumont is in the foreground, her hands held together, as if in prayer.

He lays Daddy on the altar, of course — the video went viral instantly, everyone has seen it. And instead of lifting the Applebee's-branded apple-red and green-apple-green sacrificial scabbard, he holds his father's arm steady as the medic inserts the IV cannula, then leans over and whispers in his father's ear. No one knows exactly what he says at that moment. There have been various reports. Journalist Véronique de Bernard, who was mere feet from the platform, told *Inside Triathlon* readers that he said either "Run your race" or "You've done your pace," while other earwitnesses have suggested alternatives ("I'll wash your face," say, or "How does this taste?"). Memes and T-shirts with these slogans and other variations are everywhere. For his part, despite the sponsorship offers and licensing deals on the table, Junior isn't telling, while Daddy — he can't remember a thing.

"Technically, Junior, I won."
   "I'm beginning to think you just like to complain."
   "I'm just saying: technically, *I crossed the finish line first."*
   "Uh-huh."
   "You were carrying me in your arms, therefore, clearly, I crossed the finish line first."
   "Fine. You won. Congrats."
   "Ergo…"
   "Yes?"
   "Ergo, I get to kill you."
   "Maybe next time, Daddy."
   "Hmmmph."
   "What?"
   "You say 'next time' every time."
   "C'est la guerre, Daddy."
   "That's it then, Junior?"
   "That's it."
   "This is goodbye?"
   "For now, yes; goodbye."
   "Leaving me here to —"
   "You'll be perfectly fine."
   "I should have killed you when I had the chance."

"Daddy, please. We settled that. Besides, you've got it made here. Pretty nurses everywhere, catering to your every whim..."

"I don't want to die. This is the shits; it really is."

"I know, Daddy. But this is how it goes. You run and run and run."

"And?"

"And then you stop, Daddy. You run and run and run. And then you stop." Junior leaned forward and kissed his father's head. Then he stood to go. "I'm going now."

"So go already."

"Goodbye, Daddy."

"Goodbye, you miserable fruit of my loins."

"I love you."

"I know. Stop reminding me."

Erik sat on the stack of phone books and tried to stop himself from crying. He'd been crying a lot lately, almost anything could set him off. He knew he was upset about his parents' split, but it wasn't just that. Sometimes he cried when he felt happy or when he was listening to iTunes and heard a song he really liked. Maybe the lyrics would set him off, maybe a sad chord change. Stupid things. Sometimes there was no reason; nothing happened, he just cried.

This time, he felt like crying almost as soon as he got in the garage. They'd rock-paper-scissored for dibs on the shed, and Jackson came up paper to Erik's rock.

Red Firebird

The weird part was that Erik *knew* Jackson was going to play paper, and he had rocked even though he knew he shouldn't. Still, it was no big deal. Jackson had asked him to help and he was bored and didn't mind helping and would have done it even if Jackson hadn't offered to go halves with the money. There was something about the garage, though, that made him sad. Maybe it was all the boxes of junk. It was like seeing all the moments from a person's life scattered in front of you. The things that seemed important once, now packed in damp boxes, waiting to be picked through by strangers or thrown away.

There was also the car, the cherry-red Firebird, an antique almost. In another situation, this car might have made Erik feel happy. It was very shiny and had chrome wheels and looked like the kind of car you would make with a model kit when you were a kid. But here, now, it was just kind of creepy. How the old lady could keep it, Erik didn't know. Her husband had killed himself in that car, Jackson'd told him; run a vacuum hose from the exhaust pipe to the interior, used plastic garbage bags and duct tape to make a perfect seal.

Erik wondered how long Mr. Wallace had sat there, waiting for the fumes to take effect. Maybe he'd brought a bottle of something in with him — rye was Erik's guess. Old men liked rye. Maybe he had drunk a few glasses of rye first or taken some pills? In any case, it freaked Erik out to think that someone had died in the garage. Erik was the kind of person that believed in ghosts and zombies and other supernatural shit like that, and he could not help but feel that the old man's ghost — his *Ba* — was there, watching, maybe pissed off that this stranger was going through all his stuff deciding what to keep, what to sell and what to throw away.

But that's not what made him cry. It was something stupid. There was a big cardboard box sitting on a broken chest of drawers at the very far end of the garage. *Oregon State Apples*, the box read. He was drawn to it for some reason; he felt there was something important in it. Erik went directly over to the box and crouched down a bit to get himself set. He expected it to be heavy, and he didn't want to hurt his back. But when he picked the box up, he almost fell backwards, it was so light.

Erik set the box on the empty workbench and unfolded the lid. There was a single hat in the box. It was an old man's fedora, greenish-brown like a lake trout, a red and grass-green fishing fly stuck in the band. That's what made him cry, the idea of the hat, by itself, at the bottom of the cardboard box. Stupid.

And that's when he sat down on the stack of phone books, holding the hat in both hands, trying not to cry, taking deep, slow breaths just like the school counsellor had shown him. He'd catch his breath for a moment, slow down his breathing, feel a sense of control, then lose it again, sobbing and gasping. Eventually, he calmed down. He sat there trying not to think of the image of the hat in the box and trying also not to think about the stack of phone books he was sitting on (the thought that someone could not even bring themselves to throw away a phone book made him sad in a different way). After a while, he forgot about trying not to cry. All he could think about now was trying the hat on. Somehow he felt it would be wrong to wear the hat, that maybe the old man's spirit would see him and get angry, or that maybe the old man had been wearing that hat when he died, and that by putting it on, Erik might somehow be inviting death into his life. He thought about that a lot lately: death. It terrified him. He hoped the Egyptians were right, that there was an afterworld where you kind of just carried on like you did now, only better. Or maybe there was something even bigger going on, like Solonnikov said. If ancient aliens were real, then anything was possible. And that made him happy for a moment, to think that anything was possible. When you got right down to it, that's all he'd been thinking about lately; the possible and the impossible, and the possible was kind of like life, and the impossible was kind of like the other alternative. The forever of death, without the actual death.

Erik could feel his heart beat as he picked the hat up and placed it on his head. Of course, the hat fit perfectly. He knew that it would. He hopped off the stack of phone books and squeezed himself between the wall and the Firebird. He bent down to check himself out in the side-view mirror. He didn't always look good in a hat, he really didn't have the head for certain kinds of hats, but this hat looked great. He decided he liked it and that he would ask Mrs. Wallace if he could keep it. It would be great in the Zombie Apocalypse. He could see himself in that hat, driving around the city in the cherry-red Firebird, pumping both barrels of a shotgun into the head of any zombie that tried to get in his way. In his mind's eye, he could see the zombie heads exploding, spraying brains and skin and blood and skull fragments everywhere.

Erik looked out the small window above the side door. He could see Jackson, his hair wet from the persistent drizzle, bent over in the shed. Jackson had been inviting him over a lot lately, which was cool because he liked Jackson. The only thing he didn't like was Jackson's dad. Ray gave him the creeps. Sometimes you'd come over and you could tell he'd been drinking. He'd be super-happy and slurring his words and get all touchy-feely and put his arm around you. Erik's dad said Ray was an alcoholic. That's why he kept getting fired, Erik's dad said. Erik wasn't sure whether to believe his dad or not — his dad was one of those people who thought everyone was an alcoholic, probably because his own dad, Erik's grandfather, had been a serious alcoholic who drank himself to death, his father said, before Erik was even born. One morning, though, Erik and his dad were parked at a strip mall on the way to Portland, waiting for Dolly, Erik's sister, to finish up her hair appointment at the Art of Style. They were sitting in the front seat playing bloody knuckles when Erik's dad said, *Shit, there's Ray.* Jackson's dad was standing in front of Wine World, even though it wasn't even ten o'clock yet. For some reason that Erik never quite understood — perhaps just because it was fun — he and his dad slid down in their car seats, like they were spies or cops on a stakeout. They secretly watched Ray. He was the first one in the liquor store when it opened its doors, and the first guy out a few minutes later, a case of Schlitz under each arm. They watched Ray get into his car. He popped one of the cans before he even got his seat belt on.

"Jesus," Erik's dad had said. "It's not even quarter past ten."

Erik saw Ray pour the beer into one of those coffee travel mugs, take another sip, then put his seat belt on. He drove right past Erik and his dad on the way out of the mall, but he was too busy looking around to notice them.

Jackson was bending down again. He was going through a box of stuff, pool toys it looked like, even though Mrs. Wallace didn't have a pool. It's weird how people collected things throughout their lives, unnecessary things like joke gifts they were given at an office party or junk they'd picked up at a garage sale, those things that just magically appeared in your house and became part of the landscape, useless and unseen, until someone got an urge to clean. It was funny how people became attached to things. His mother had a collection of Japanese teacups, even though she had never been to Japan and never drank tea. His grandmother collected spoons from all over the world. Anytime anyone went anywhere, Erik's grandma would say, *Don't forget to bring me back a spoon.* They weren't even real spoons, just little tourist ones, too small for anything but maybe stirring the invisible tea in his mother's cups.

Jackson was standing up now and stretching, putting his hands on the small of his back and bending backwards, so that he looked kind of like a rooster or an athlete warming up. He was wearing sweatpants that were very tight and, now that they were wet from the rain, clung to him real tight. Erik caught himself looking at Jackson's ass. Sometimes Erik worried that he might be gay, because he often found himself staring at guys' asses and chests and stuff and getting a little turned on. But he knew he wasn't gay, because he also looked at girls' tits and asses, and sometimes just doing that would get him super-hard. So who knows? One time at a party these guys, Derek and Jamie, made out for like five minutes on a dare and later Jackson, who was pretty drunk, told him that he thought it was kind of hot. Maybe everybody was a little gay like that? Maybe staring at another guy's ass and getting a little turned on was normal. Maybe not everything fit into perfect categories, like you were led to believe.

Erik put his elbows on the ledge of the little window. Sometimes he thought it would be cool if he and Jackson were together in the Zombie Apocalypse. They'd fight the zombies together, like brothers, and maybe live in the samehouse and be best friends or brothers. Maybe they'd sleep in the same bed at night. Erik liked the thought of that. It'd be cool, like a sleepover every night. He would like to have a best friend like that, and even though he knew the Zombie Apocalypse wasn't exactly a real thing, he still thought it would be cool to be in the Zombie Apocalypse with Jackson.

Across the garage another container caught his eye. It was at the bottom of a stack of crooked cardboard boxes, and made of light blue plastic. It stood out, and Erik had a feeling that whatever was in it was probably important. Jackson was walking across the backyard now, heading toward the house, carrying a huge snowman Christmas ornament. Erik smiled and waved with both hands and pointed at the hat on his head, but Jackson didn't see him.

The cardboard boxes on top of the blue container were full of paperback books, mostly old science-fiction and detective novels right out of the 1970s. Erik dug through the first couple boxes, looking for something interesting, but nothing caught his eye. So he picked up the rest of the boxes two at a time and carried them over to the workbench. Finally, he got to the blue container. He slid it to the centre of the garage and lifted the lid. At first, it seemed like he'd made a mistake. There didn't seem to be anything much in it. Just a couple car manuals on the top and some shoe boxes and stuff. He opened one box and found a bunch of documents that looked like bank stuff and legal papers. They might have been important. He set that box aside; Mrs. Wallace might need some of those papers. He pulled out another box and opened the lid — and seriously almost dropped it. There was a tube of KY on top of a stack of really old video tapes, obviously pornos: *Nasty Neighbors VI, Anal 3Somes, Raw and Dirty* and so on. Stuffed into one side of the box was a baggie with rolling papers in it and what looked like some weed. He unsealed the baggie and took a whiff. Definitely pot.

Erik couldn't get his head around any of it. He'd never met Mr. Wallace, but he was definitely a really old guy and couldn't have possible been into pot. And the porn? Erik was pretty sure old people didn't watch pornos. Maybe this guy was just a dirty old man? Maybe it was just what you *think* you know about people is never the same as what a person is actually like; maybe most people kept parts of themselves hidden away in little boxes? Then Erik felt super-embarrassed. He felt like he was totally invading this old guy's privacy, wearing his hat, looking at his hidden porn, eyeballing his pot stash.

Erik opened the lid on another shoebox. There were letters in it, all folded up, and the vague smell of perfume. He decided right away he would not read the letters, that would be going too far, but he felt around in the box, really because he was hoping to find some more pot. He felt something that wasn't a letter and pulled out a few photographs. He only had time to glimpse at the top one — a bald man lying on a bed naked, with a naked woman on each side of him — when he heard Jackson calling outside.

Erik threw the pictures back in the box and pushed the lid back on. But Jackson wasn't calling his name; he was calling for his mom and it sounded like he was running back to his house as he did it.

Erik listened carefully. But nothing. He opened the shoebox again and picked up the photos. There were three of them, and they all looked like they'd been taken at the same time. There were the same three people in all of them: a bald man and two women, one redhead, one blonde. In the first picture, the women were lying beside the bald guy, touching his privates although he wasn't hard or anything. In the second picture, they were on their knees on either side of him, leaning over his chest, kissing each other. The bald guy was hard in that one. The third picture was mostly out of focus, the bald guy, from behind, having sex with the redhead, whose face was buried under the blonde, who was basically sitting on her.

The people were old, like in their thirties, and Erik wondered if the bald man was Mr. Wallace and if maybe one of the women, the redhead maybe, was his wife. And even though he felt like a total perv for doing it, he started to rub himself through his pants. He knew the people in the pictures were old at the time, and were now probably old men and women like Mrs. Wallace, if not dead, but he couldn't help but get turned on. He felt super-guilty unzipping his pants and was worried too that he might get caught, which would have been totally embarrassing. He thought about going over and locking the garage door, but he was pretty sure that no one could see him anyway, even if they burst right in; there were too many boxes and shit in the way. He knew he had to hurry. There was some kind of commotion going on in the backyard. He could hear someone banging on the back door of Mrs. Wallace's house, and someone, it sounded like Jackson's mom, was yelling Mrs. Wallace's name. Erik pulled his pants and underwear down to his knees and felt the cold concrete floor against his ass. He tilted his head back and focused on the photos of the ladies kissing, which he held up with his free hand, and tried not to think of Mr. Wallace's ghost, which could be, for all he knew, stuck inside the red Firebird, inches away, watching everything he was doing and trying to figure how to reach across from the River of Death and stop this stranger from wearing his hat and stealing all these little pieces of his life.

It was the perfect dish for falling in love. Light and hot and sublime, a first kiss, the vegetables still crisp, the fish itself fleshy and moist and just fishy enough to remind you of what you were eating.

Not the perfect meal, mind you. The melon gazpacho was obscene, the antipasto was pulpy and had come, no doubt, from a can. The juustoleipa with wild strawberries, while daring (and taken on its own merits, rather inspired), just sat there on its own, an afterthought or ellipsis (and not a period full stop, marking the end of the meal). But the entree...a brill moqueca on a nopal pizzoccheri. Everything in harmony:

The Art of Fine Eating

crunchy, smooth, sweet undertones and the drone of something (nutmeg? It sounded inconceivable, but there it was) that drew the entire dish together. It was the pimenta malagueta, of course, that added the zip (what love affair could start without a little heat?), but the real surprise was the coconut sorbet (just a tease, though, which won Paul over; coconut, he maintained, should only be used sparingly, like a spice). It languished on the bed of steaming Portuguese beans and unfolded in the heat like lazy foreplay.

"The plating leaves much to be desired..."

Vivian nodded her agreement, while the manner in which she drew the fork from her mouth told him that she was savouring the dish as much as he.

Paul liked the way she ate. He had already decided that. Eating, like cooking, was an art, and all art required balance. The trick to preparing a great dish was geometrical, almost architectural, measuring shapes and sizes and constructing them in a way that was structurally sound, functional and aesthetically appealing. The trick to great eating was much more sublime and therefore vastly more difficult: one must perform the basest of animal functions while maintaining the illusion of semi-divinity. Vivian did this and more. She achieved the effect, Paul surmised, by careful attention to posture and angles, sitting just enough on her chair as to be drawn forward toward him at all times (creating the illusion — there's that word again — of delicate stability), and careful use of props. The knife and fork performed a subtle ritual, never completely touching each other or the plate or her lips, the two never breaking his plane of view at the same time.

Afterwards they walked the causeway. The night was warm and the sky had turned the colour of fresh arancini as the last of the sunlight melted away. Paul boldly took her hand.

"They call it scattering, the meteorologists... Dust and other aerosols — pollution, I suppose — deflect the light waves..." Often, in moments of great intimacy, he found himself running off at the mouth. A nervous tic.

Once again, Vivian nodded. "Red sky at night, sailor's delight; red sky at dawn, sailor's forewarn? Is that it?" She laughed, suddenly self-conscious, and squeezed his hand.

"It's close enough," he replied, suppressing the urge to kiss her. That would come later, as they sat on the bench near the end of the walkway, warming themselves in the ricotta moon and discussing the intricacies of the perfect burro bercy. Vivian edged her head onto his shoulder and tilted her eyes up until he had no choice. Paul drew forward as she took his chin in her small hand. At first, her lips barely touched his, creating a kind of electrical anticipation, and as her fingers lightly touched his face, and her lips and breath passed microscopically close to his skin, he found himself *sol punto di scoppiare* and feeling already a little bit in love.

Vivian had a good job with a sturdy human resources consulting firm. She had her own condominium and two cats. She had been engaged once but it had not worked out. The man, apparently a cad of the highest order (those are exactly the words she used), had slept with her best friend while Vivian was off in Boston visiting her elderly mother. This is what he knew of her before the first kiss.

They had met on an Internet dating site called Food Lovers, "Where Passion and Food Meet." Paul was just browsing, having stumbled upon the site while looking up information on Tuscan wines of the exceptional 1997 vintage. He signed in, using his editor's email address, and visited the chat room, which featured rather less discussion of food and rather more flirtation buried under the weight of double entendre and chat-room shorthand. And while he made a poor peeping Tom, he did discover Vivian's profile. It featured a photo of a tanned woman, her brown hair drawn back by a yellow ribbon, standing in a yellow kitchen, a blue-and-white-checkered apron around her waist, one fist resting on each hip. Her head was turned, which made her look modest and sexy at the same time. It was an unposed snapshot, slightly blurred at the edges, which would not have looked out of place in a *Good Housekeeping* ad for electric ranges, circa 1953. In her turn-ons, she listed fine dining, wine, travel and books; turnoffs included raw tomatoes, Scrabble, facial hair and Adam Sandler movies. She sounded perfect. And so — what the hell — he sent her a text, and waited. He was patient, mind, surmising (correctly) that an attractive woman listed on an Internet dating site would likely have a lot of chaff to sift through. Even then, when she read his text, would she bother to respond? Perhaps she'd see a glimmer of something in his note. Was that enough? Surely, if the Internet had taught the world anything, it was that one should keep one's expectations low and hope for the occasional miracle.

It wasn't exactly a whirlwind romance, but it was very comfortable. They were no spring chickens, after all. She still maintained her book club and calligraphy class and had recently signed up to study Falun Gong with a girlfriend; Paul had his baseball fantasy pool and night-school Italian. And if readers of "Haute and Bothered," his weekly restaurant review column, noticed any difference, they did not comment. Paul himself made a conscious effort to avoid sounding overly ebullient; love had that effect on him, as his editor at the Chronicle reminded him: "You're vinegar, Paul, Rubio balsamic, aged to perfection, but vinegar all the same. That's what the readers want."

Jackson was kibitzing, of course, but Paul got the hint. His very next review (Con Amore!) was savoury and not the least bit sweet: *the duck was the culinary equivalent of trailer trash, all fat and completely lacking in taste, while the pine-nut gnocchi was bitter and dry with a rank Puttanesca sauce, which, despite its namesake, did not go down easy…*

Vivian now accompanied him on all his restaurant visits. She was initially surprised that he would always call ahead, giving his victims (again, that was her term), every chance to prepare. And while she herself was no expert on food (despite or perhaps because of her half-Calabrian grandmother), she knew what she liked and was able to overcome her innate niceness to be a perfect conduit into the hearts and stomachs of his readers, *la gente comune*.

Food, then, became the major point of contact in their lives, or more correctly, their shared life, for as Paul realized, his world had so perfectly folded into Vivian's that there was no longer a distinction between the two. They had entered unmistakable couplehood (confirming his suspicion that he was, deep down, inherently lovable and her belief that there was indeed hope for women over forty) without ever sacrificing their selves.

For the sake of precision, it would be more correct to say that *eating* had become the major contact point. The difference was subtle but significant. She knew nothing about the Northern Italian food he loved so deeply, of *la Cucina del Trentino Alto Adige* or *la Cucina del Friuli Venezia Giulia* or *Piemontese* or *Trentino Alto Adige* or any of the communal cuisines that marked each place as surely as any border, geographical or political. Meanwhile, her general knowledge of culinary arts was limited to reruns of Iron Chef, half-forgotten sorties in high school home ec class decades before and the occasional Learning Annex workshop (Sushi for Beginners, The Joy of Wine, etc.). He was not by nature a pedant, and she, while genuinely interested, was not one to sit idly through a one-sided conversation. So instead they talked about what they did like and what they didn't and why. And Paul watched her eat. The fork, simply resting on her fingertips, the knife suspended between her thumb and forefinger, held by an invisible rivet, and nothing, again, completely touching anything else; a sleight of hand. Her tongue was always perfectly moist as it rose to meet the food, extending beyond the lips just far enough to seem erotic: a micrometre further, the scene would have collapsed into burlesque; a hair's breadth shorter and her tongue would have seemed untonguely. Reptilian.

A simple egg dish marked the beginning of the end. Frittata alle salsiccia, lightly herbed with ground rosemary and dried thyme. Uncomplicated, austere; in hindsight, quite fitting. Of course, at the time they thought it was nothing. A loss of appetite, nothing more. A touch of stomach flu or even food poisoning (he'd warned her about leftover chicken, but you can't turn off a lifetime of frugality just like that). She barely touched her eggs. Two weeks later and her appetite had not returned. A CAT scan confirmed her doctor's worst suspicions: exocrine pancreatic cancer. Although it was already at the T2 stage, which meant tumour cells had spread to the duodenum and bile duct, the oncologist sounded optimistic.

"This is a very aggressive form of cancer, although your wife is still relatively young."

Paul smiled slightly at the physician's mistake; he was certain Vivian would get a kick out of it too. The doctor had a heavy Asian accent, which distracted Paul for a moment. He thought of the Eight Great Culinary Traditions of China and, trying to remember them all, got stuck at six. He made a mental note to google the other two when he got home.

The doctor suggested a forceful counterattack, starting with what he called the Whipple procedure, which involved removing part of the pancreas along with other impacted organs (which, in this case, the doctor believed, would include the duodenum and perhaps gall bladder), followed by twelve weeks of chemotherapy. When he opened her up, though, he discovered that the tumour had spread to the colon and stomach. He stitched her up again and cautioned friends and family to make their peace.

Paul was there when the doctor spoke to Vivian. Her head was propped up with two pillows, and the room had that sweet and vaguely fecal hospital smell — Nilodor and soiled sheets. Paul held her hand as the doctor bluntly laid it out: six weeks, perhaps eight. Three months at the very most.

"The cancer is metastasizing at a rapid rate; we could put out a little fire here only to have another start there. We can't stop it, but we can do our best to make you comfortable."

There was measured reason to the oncologist's words, and Paul felt himself calmed. After the doctor left, Paul suggested they get some Chinese food to go. Vivian smiled and said that that would be nice.

"Nothing too spicy, I suppose. Hunan? Jiangsu? Shandong?"

Vivian waved her hand. She would leave it up to him.

There was a lightness to his step, which belied the circumstances. It had occurred to him: he'd never seen her eat with chopsticks. He could only imagine it would be delightful.

The oncologist was not being optimistic. Six weeks less a day from his diagnosis, Vivian succumbed. Her last real meal, taken eight days before her passing, was simple peasant fare, prepared especially by the head chef at Vecchia Trattoria: warm polenta with gorgonzola, sautéed spinach and roasted pumpkin seeds. *Il cibo dell'anima*: food for the soul. And even in her weakened state, Vivian managed to attain a certain poise. She was too weak to hold the utensils on her own or to sit up properly, but he had adjusted the bed and, with the nurse's help, had placed pillows under her head, back and knees. She looked perfect.

"Simple food need not be lousy food, eh?" He held another forkful to Vivian's mouth, before realizing that she was still chewing absently. It was an effort for her to swallow, and the act sent her into a violent spasm of coughing. He grabbed the water cup from the bedside table and pressed the straw to her lips.

"I'm thinking of writing an entire book devoted to peasant food," Paul said, though her coughing fit had not fully subsided. "A recipe book of sorts, but part history and part philosophy..."

Paul had a theory. The way he saw it, eating had become an industrial process in American culture, and food a simple commodity. Even the latest obsession with the culinary arts — with twenty-four-hour cable channels devoted to fine dining and chefs morphing into media superstars, expensive coffee-table books and glossy magazines — all this was just a fashion. *Food as elegant product, but product nonetheless.*

"In Asian and European cultures, eating is still celebrated. People gather together, not to consume a product, but to celebrate life, and engage in a kind of holy communion with food at its heart…"

Vivian pursed her lips and turned her head away.

"Done? But you've barely touched your polenta, *pucci.*" Vivian closed her eyes, and he understood. Now, she needed to rest; the food, she could finish later.

There were no famous last words. For a week or so she drifted in and out of consciousness; distracted by pain, seduced by slow starvation and the morphine drip, she would emerge every so often to turn abruptly and mutter some sounds that couldn't have been meant for anyone but the shades in her dreams. The whole thing unfolded without drama, just a kind of orderly undoing, supervised by the hospice nurses. The night Vivian died, the very moment was, as the Poet said, an art as natural as eating. Her breathing, which had been slow and very deep, suddenly changed, a succession of staccato breaths that grew shorter but more separate. And then she opened her eyes, looking at once at him and through him. Her lips were dry and pursed, but she licked them softly with her soft tongue, and for a moment her face brightened as if she were about to say something sparkling. She sat like that, on the verge of something, then slowly, slowly, closed her eyes again.

The funeral was a catered affair, a ghastly montage of coconut shrimp, jerk-chicken skewers and salt-lick meatballs impaled on tiny plastic swords. During the service, Paul felt awkward and stood at the back of the chapel, despite the encouragement of two of Vivian's girlfriends, who urged him to take a seat at the front pew.

Paul pursed his lips and forced himself to breathe slowly, as his therapist had instructed, when the minister mentioned him by name. In was only a passing reference, the minister giving thanks for the companionship Paul had provided Vivian the last few months of her life, and broadly hinting that the two were planning to become engaged sometime in the indeterminate future. He felt bodies shift and eyes scour the room in search of the unfortunate, bereaved fiancé-to-be. Breathe, he told himself, breathe.

At the end of the service, he quietly introduced himself to Vivian's mother. She looked up at him from her wheelchair and smiled, but held a vacant look in her eyes: she had no idea who he was. Toby, Vivian's only sibling, had only just arrived from New York. A merchant banker, tall and very lank, he looked nothing like his sister. He was polite as could be expected, and although both had been intimately connected to Vivian, neither man succumbed to a false sense of attachment to the other. Toby introduced Paul to everyone as "my sister's boyfriend," a term that sounded transitional if not downright seedy under the circumstances.

"How long had the two of you been dating?" asked some weathered friend of an aunt, stumbling a moment over the tense. That was always the difficult one at a service like this, finding the balance between good manners and grammatical precision.

"We met nine months ago."

"She is . . . was a lovely girl."

"Yes. Indeed."

The woman had pressed him for further details of their relationship. Where had they met? Were they planning to marry? Have children? Buy a house? There was a persistence to the woman, which one could have interpreted, Paul believed, as hostility.

Paul felt a funny sense that people were watching him as he conversed with this woman. He needed something to do with his hands, and absently grabbed an appetizer off the tray of a passing waiter.

"It's a terrible shame. The cancer. I saw her only a few months ago, and everything was fine."

Paul nodded politely. "It was all so sudden."

"So very sudden. She was fine one day, and the next day..."

"At least, she didn't suffer," Paul said, still nodding endlessly and waving the appetizer — smoked tuna on a Triscuit — without ever actually taking a bite.

"It was the same with my Harold." She lowered her voice, as if they were conspirators. "Bowel cancer. They kept cutting pieces of it out of him until there was nothing left."

"I'm sorry — are you saying he did suffer?"

"Oh yes. It was horrible. The pain and, of course, the incontinence..."

He managed to distract the woman with a passing plate of California rolls, and quickly made his escape. He stood for a moment by the buffet table at the back of the chapel hall, but the sight of that food, glaring at him, only caused further distress. Paul felt his head grow hot and sweat rising around the back of his neck. His breathing grew more laboured and he felt the overwhelming need to leave.

Later, at Fresco, he treated himself to a bottle of Brunello di Montalcino and contemplated the menu. He was trying to decide, not what to eat, but why he was eating. What was the event? Had he come to celebrate Vivian's life or mourn her passing? Was this their last meal together or the first meal of a new chapter of his life?

"Dining alone tonight, sir?"

Paul nodded, gently, and the waiter removed the other service from the table. Paul considered staying his hand. Maybe he could pour a glass of wine for her, or at least for her memory? But no. That would seem quite strange — Fresco was the kind of place where the waiters wore white aprons, with elegant booths and white linen table-cloths — not to mention a waste of good wine.

He would drink to her memory. That was more in keeping with the time and place. "What can you recommend?"

"Everything is good tonight, sir. But if I may suggest, the pappardelle with a duck and wild mushroom ragout…"

That was to Paul's liking, and as the waiter removed the extra cutlery and glassware, he leaned back in his chair and let out a long breath. He felt his shoulders relax, and lifted the Brunello to his nose. Through the window, he could see the sun slipping beneath the hills in the distance, turning the sky the colour of a blood orange.

The waiter returned with a basket of hot focaccia. He picked up Paul's heavy napkin and unfurled it in a single, studied motion. He laid the napkin on Paul's lap. For a moment, their arms touched.

Paul tore a piece of bread and reached forward to dip it in a saucer of oil and vinegar, knocking his wineglass with his suit sleeve. It didn't quite spill — the waiter was there to catch it before any damage was done, although a tiny portion, no more than a few drops really, splashed onto the linen. The marks were somewhat unsettling, but Paul didn't say anything. After all, it was his fault. He was clumsy, that was all. Not thoughtless or careless. Food he knew, portion and proportion and structure and the blending of tastes — this he understood, just as he understood that there would always be spills and crumbs and stains on the napkin and little dollops of sauce dripping from his chin. And at the end of the meal, the waiter would bring him a hot towel, and he would wipe his fingers and face, and ball the towel up, then unball it and fold it neatly and lay it on his empty plate. And it would be in the taxi home that night that the sadness would hit him, and he would feel, for the first time, almost like crying. Not for the loss he had suffered, that was bound to happen, but for the things unsaid and the meals never to be eaten, and for the sudden understanding that, of all the things he might achieve before he died, he would never fully master the art of fine eating.

Jasper won a hundred dollars on the scratch-and-win and took them all to the indoor water park. There was a small pool that Mose could play in with its own little slide that went in and out of a fibreglass waterfall and a seahorse he could sit on and press a button and make water shoot out of the seahorse's head. There was a giant wave pool and seven different slides. Every ten minutes a foghorn would sound, and the waves would come, getting bigger and bigger until when Diane was at the top of one wave she couldn't even seen Birdy, paddling like mad, at the bottom of another.

Lenny and Oliver had come too, just for the hell of it.

Arrivederci Homos

"I could use a day at the beach," Oliver said, and Lenny, who seemed even more stoned than usual, came along for the ride.

Oliver was wearing a T-shirt that he'd won on a cruise ship — green, white and red like the Italian flag, with the phrase *Arrivederci Homos* in big letters on the back. They'd been at the pool about an hour when a manager came over and asked Lenny to take the shirt off.

"Some of the patrons are finding it offensive." The manager was not much older than Jasper. You could tell that asking people to take off offensive T-shirts was not a part of the job he liked.

"Offensive?"

Oliver was close to losing it. Diane hoped he'd just take the shirt off. Everybody was having so much fun, and she didn't want them to get kicked out.

"It's, you know, homophobic."

"But *I'm* gay." Oliver was almost yelling now.

The manager turned red almost right away. He looked like he might start to cry. He walked away without saying anything else.

In a while, a girl from the concession came over with ice cream cones and popcorn. She gave Oliver an envelope with five free passes in it. When Oliver opened the envelope and saw the passes, he put his hand over his heart and Diane could see he was tearing up. Oliver was pretty flamboyant and theatrical, even for a gay guy, but Diane felt sorry for him. He must've felt real bad for almost yelling at the manager.

Later, Oliver turned his T-shirt inside out. Lenny got mad at him and told him how he shouldn't give in to authority and how this wasn't a police state and how Oliver had the right to wear anything he wanted on a T-shirt and how Oliver should lodge a complaint against the waterslide people with the Human Rights Commission. But Oliver seemed happy enough, and all the way on the bus ride home he kept saying how much he loved a day at the beach.

A massive storm is hitting the Eastern Seaboard, a black cloud of dust extending some four hundred miles and carrying with it an estimated 650 million tons of debris. Some parts of Chicago and Boston have seen up to nine inches of dust accumulate overnight, while the death toll in New York City exceeds 1,200, mostly the elderly, the poor or the homeless. The mayor has closed the ports and is declaring an official state of emergency.

The West Coast, while not hit as hard, is experiencing black snow as an Arctic cold front moves in from the north and mixes with the falling dust. Frozen crystals, the colour of a dirty latte, have been coming down since lunchtime, disrupting Michael and Andrew's wedding preparations

Still Life with Birds and Dust

and, by bringing the city's already-compromised transport system to a standstill, causing them to consider postponing the ceremony altogether.

"Let me ask you something, Andrew. Are you getting married because you are in love with me and want to share the rest of your life with me or because you are in love with me and feel the need to make a political statement?"

"That's a hell of a question to ask someone, Michael."

They stand in front of the vacant lot between a Fuddruckers hamburger franchise and a Texaco service station, a steel tang to the air, watching two seagulls battle a crow over a strip of plastic wrap. They are curious-looking gulls, smaller than normal, with round black heads. Michael, who had helped his children through a "bird phase" when they were younger, correctly identifies them as Bonaparte's gulls. One gull is holding the plastic in its beak as the other one stands close, assuming a defensive posture, wings unfurled in sharp, pointed Vs, head back, cawing staccato threats at the wary crow. The crow pecks now and then, stabbing at the precious garbage. Michael notices that the crow has a deformed foot, the talon curled in a permanent fist. He wavers, one moment rooting for the ambitious crow, the next for the persistent, valiant gulls.

"Fact: Bonaparte's gull is named not after the famous emperor, but his nephew, Charles Lucien Jules Laurent Bonaparte."

Andrew is holding his arm, wipes away the dust accumulating on Michael's shoulder. He is almost fifty-seven, Michael, although the official biography on the university website shaves off five years.

"One of the most celebrated ornithologists of his day, Charles Bonaparte's achievements include the discovery of two bird species, the moustached warbler and the Wilson's storm petrel, the description and classification of one hundred more species and the creation of the genus *Zenaida, named in honour of his wife and first cousin,* Zénaïde Laetitia Julie Bonaparte."

Michael watches. The crow gives up and flies off, slow, sulky wing strokes. The bird passes close to them and lands on top of the temporary fence. It perches for a moment, then lets out a string of accusatory caws.

"You are a veritable fountain of information, Dr. Wiess."

"I am trying to stay relevant."

Dry soil is piled across the lot, and each mound covered by a blue tarp held in place with cinder blocks. Michael is tall and thin and still wears a suit and tie when he gives a lecture, a practice his colleagues abandoned long ago. He tries to remember the building that stood on this spot years before. The Chinese Public School, he thinks, with its multi-tiered, overhanging gable roof, sweeping curves and upturned eaves.

"They're putting up a Target Superstore," Andrew says, wiping at the thin layer of dust coating his goggles. Andrew is thirty-one and, perhaps because he is a little stocky or because of his thin beard and serious spectacles or because of his penchant for cardigan sweaters, he is often mistaken for a much older man.

Michael nods. He has never been to a Target, and although he is not much of a shopper and has an irrational opposition to big-box stores, he feels a sense of anticipation that borders on excitement at the idea of having a Target Superstore this close to his home. He feels Andrew's arm around his shoulder.

"What should we do today, Professor?"

"I thought we'd get married, Andrew."

"And then?"

"And then our life will begin."

The dust storms started the previous spring. The last few winters have been mild and abnormally dry, extending a drought that began almost two years earlier. Wildfires have raged through the coastal and mountain forests, while heat waves have scorched the grassy plains and rangelands. Still, scientists are not able to pinpoint the exact cause of the dust storms. The usual suspects — global warming, solar flares, the dawning ice age, capitalist greed, God's vengeance — have all been cited, but nothing quite explains why massive clouds of dust are rolling across the continent.

It's a wonder they can fly at all, the gulls, the crows. The dust is taking its toll. You see dead birds everywhere, lying at the base of every building, their necks broken from unexpected impacts, or tottering at the side of the road like drunken nuns, trying to recoordinate their wings. It isn't just their lungs that are affected — no doubt the coarse dust is slowly choking the birds from the inside — but other physical functions too: scar tissue is building up on their eyes, making it difficult for them to navigate and find food, while the delicate chemicals of their inner ears are clogging, impairing the birds' sense of balance and direction. Ornithologists across the continent report that flocks of geese and other waterfowl are flying west and east and north for the winter — anywhere but south — travelling in large concentric circles or jagged-lightning flight paths, desperate to migrate but no longer able to tune in to the Earth's magnetic fields for guidance. Scientists recently tracked one flock of snow geese that left Frobisher Bay and travelled 2,700 miles along a circuitous route, only to wind up in Washington, D.C., eight weeks later in the midst of a severe ice storm. Nearly seven hundred birds froze to death on the steps of the Lincoln Memorial.

Of course, birds are not the only animals being affected. Cows, horses, even deer and other wild ungulates, are dying on their feet, their complex digestive systems blocked and riddled with ulcers, while large carnivores and omni-vores, like the various species of bear and wild canines — wolves, coyotes, even certain foxes — are succumbing to a dust-induced rabies, which, although neither viral-based nor contagious, causes the kind of acute encephalitis and associate symptoms (hyperkinesis, hydrophobia, incipient mania) characteristic of a full-blown rabies attack. Reports of the rabies are widespread, and there is significant cir-cumstantial evidence linking the disorder to climatic irreg-ularities (outbreaks of the so-called Brager's rabies, named for the Norwegian researcher who first identified it, are thirty-seven per cent more likely to occur in areas that have experienced high to severe dust accumulations over the previous nine months), scientists have yet to describe the exact etiology of the disease.

Perhaps no other animal is more adversely affected than *Canis lupus familiaris*, the common domestic dog. It only stands to reason, given their near-parasitic relation-ship to humans and their general physiological disposi-tion: head down, experiencing the world nose-first. Previously rare nasal and sinus cancers are endemic, with the epithelium tissue of the paranasal sinuses — the hollow spaces in the skull — particularly susceptible. Despite the best efforts of veterinary science and com-merce — everything from specially designed surgical masks and lubricant creams to portable filtration sys-tems that cover the animal's entire head — the tide of canine carcinoma cannot be stemmed.

"I believe, Andrew, that love elevates and ennobles the human experience. And while it erupts, as the venerable Augustine

says, like an earthquake, it is not breathlessness, it is not excitement. Love itself is what is left over when being in love has burned away."

"You say very passionate things without a hint of passion."

Michael and Andrew walk along the cobblestone esplanade across from the harbour park, close, their steps in sync, but not holding hands. They'd met almost two years ago in the Faculty Club lounge, at one those infinite dean's socials honouring the university's most promising grad students, and Michael noticed Andrew (whose Master's thesis on Foucault and the semiotics of postwar queer cinema had just been accepted for publication by a major Canadian university) from a distance. Andrew was leaning over, talking to an Asian woman in a wheelchair, thoughtfully stroking the edges of his fluted champagne glass and glancing up every so often to see if Michael was still looking his way. While the university has a formal policy prohibiting faculty from dating students, Andrew was hardly some wide-eyed naïf falling into the clutches of a depraved older man. The relationship progressed without sanction or scandal.

"Marriage is the formal reckoning of love and is the greatest and most difficult of human relationships. No ceremony can create a marriage, no words, no piece of paper; marriage is created by two people who love and persevere, who speak at length and sit in silence, who support each other and forgive one another and themselves; marriage is created a brick at a time, with every laugh and every tear and every kiss and even every broken promise, because marriage is not about being perfect but about sharing your imperfections with another person."

"You should write a book, Michael. An in-depth analysis of marriage and love."

"Are you serious? Sometimes I can't tell."

It isn't just birds and dogs. The dust storms disrupt almost every aspect of daily life. Transportation and communication, the defining industries of the age, can no longer be relied on. The best one can hope for is a certain Third World competence: functionality, augmented by pre-technological ingenuity. The subways and trolley buses still run, when the mood suits them, while air travel is sporadic and planes are often forced to make unscheduled landings at whatever airport can accommodate them at the moment.

If the dust clouds have achieved anything, it is to have ushered in the end of the internal-combustion era. While electric vehicles can manage, you see abandoned at the side of every street and boulevard and highway cars, trucks, motorcycles, scooters — anything with a gas motor sits stalled or engine-seized, stripped of its organs and accessories (tires, batteries, mirrors — anything worth keeping) and left to dissolve in the incessant rain of dust. At first, civic officials dutifully towed and ticketed abandoned vehicles. But the municipal lots have long since filled with unclaimed clunkers, and the supply of unwanted cars and trucks vastly outstrips the demand to have them removed. With government no longer interested, citizens' groups have taken up the cause, and informal bands roam the streets at night, with great teams of men dissembling the fibreglass and metal carcasses with acetylene torches and crowbars, sometimes selling the parts on the black market, but just as often reconfiguring them into massive folk-art sculptures that are transforming the industrial heart of the city into something at once surreal and, in the right light, with just the right amount of dustfall or static electricity, achingly beautiful.

They are at the harbour park still, waiting for Jerome, Andrew's "artistic" friend from high school — they were the only two boys out in their senior class — who has offered to take the wedding photos. They were planning to take the pictures after the ceremony, but because Andrew has his heart set on shooting something outdoors, they are taking advantage of the break in the weather.

It is late summer, although everyone is dressed for the worst: windbreakers and long pants are mandatory these days, and most people wear safety goggles or at least wraparound sunglasses, regardless of the time of day. Many people have dust or surgical masks on, although scarves, pulled up over the face, are de rigueur.

"We are creatures of narrative. We dream in narrative, daydream in narrative, love in narrative, make love in narrative — "

"You are plagiarizing, Andrew."

"I am paraphrasing, Michael."

"It's a fine line."

"No it isn't."

The age difference has been a concern from the start. Michael had imagined awkward holiday dinners with Andrew's family, his mother eyeing him disdainfully as she wiped a smack of cranberry sauce from her lips with a paper napkin, Andrew's stepfather, a full two years Michael's junior, asking detailed questions about dust-bowl productivity and Depression era employment statistics, on the surface drawing a comparison between the economic turmoil of the Dirty Thirties and the current global ecological and financial crises, while covertly plumbing Michael's psyche to find the depth of its perversity. Andrew's friends too. Michael had imagined younger, effeminate males and a gaggle of loud and empty women, discussing fashion trends and swapping oral-sex tips, dragging him out to clubs to dance to retro-mix disco and the latest Lady Gaga tedium, which would not make him feel any younger, as it would be loudly professed to do, but merely underscoring the age difference: twenty-six years.

But his concerns whittled away. Andrew's parents, long since accustomed to their son's sexuality, welcome Michael into their home, and in fact seemed quite taken by his — there is no other word for it — *respectability*, while Andrew's social circle includes mostly attractive, intelligent young men who, if anything, suffer a general surfeit of seriousness.

In truth, the age difference helped bring them together, defining their relationship and creating an emotional shortcut to the kind of intimacy that otherwise might have taken months to achieve. In the end, it isn't the age difference that creates problems, but the age-related expectations that govern each man's perception of the other. It exasperates Andrew that his lover, who lived through Stonewall and the Bathhouse riots, who came of age during the height of the AIDS crisis, who survived and thrives in the aftermath, does not have the slightest interest in queer politics. At the same time, Michael finds Andrew's youthfulesque activism dull, if not dimwitted, and undermining of the general brilliance that originally sealed his attraction.

"Sometimes when you touch me, it doesn't feel like fingers at all. It doesn't feel like skin. It feels like something metal or maybe plastic."

Andrew has a habit of starting deep conversations in the middle.

"Why are you telling me this now?"

"I don't know. I am just thinking out loud."

Michael holds Andrew's hand tighter. He brings it to his lips and kisses Andrew's hard, cold knuckle.

"Fact: the Great Depression was exacerbated by a long period of severe drought and dust storms that ravaged North America's plains. Hardest hit was the so-called Dust Bowl, an area of roughly 100 million acres that incorporates parts of Texas, Oklahoma, New Mexico, Colorado and Kansas. In 1935 alone, the southern plains lost some 850 million tons of topsoil, and it has been estimated that during the 1930s, farmers in the Dust Bowl region lost on average six feet of top soil."

"Sometimes I think it will never end."

"The dust?"

"The dust. The uncertainty. Everything."

Michael smiles at Andrew and wipes the sand from his lips. He wanders off on his own, walking toward the beach before he stops by a stand of decorative spruce. He watches a small bulldozer build uniform piles of dust and sand. There is something insectual about the machine's efforts, a formician predetermination that Michael finds soothing. Meanwhile Andrew paces the esplanade, serial texting. They had a real knockdown battle the night before, and for some reason Michael is trying to remember the exact thing that Andrew said — something pompous and very grad school — before flying out of the house without a proper windbreaker or goggles or even a hat. He returned only minutes later, gasping for breath, apologizing as he held Michael close and cried.

"You're just scared, that's all," Michael said calmly.

"It's a big step."

"It's a very big step. But not quite as big as it seems."

Michael is trying to remember the argument when he notices a grey mass out of the corner of his eye. He ducks just as something coarse clips his head, knocking his Tilley hat to the ground. Michael instinctively covers his head with one arm and looks around just in time to see the gull coming in for another attack. He ducks again and waves his arms wildly above his head, embarrassed, believing that anyone watching his ungainly, unmanly flailing would find the scene comical. As he peeks through his arms, Michael sees the bird, a common glaucous-winged gull — its snowy head, neck and belly, its back and wings pearl grey — circle the rising piles of dust and sand.

"They must be nesting nearby." A what-appears-to-be-middle-aged woman in a kind of improvised burka nods at him in a familiar way, as if they are sharing a private joke. "It's a wonder they are nesting at all, what with the weather and such."

"Am I bleeding?" Michael rubs the sore spot in the middle of his head. "This is the last thing I need today — the *last* thing."

The woman touches his head without hesitation, and Michael feels an urge to pull away, but doesn't. She is not wearing gloves, and her fingers are soft. She seems on the verge of saying something, when she covers her head with her arms. Michael instinctively ducks. He hears a whoosh of air and feels something — talons? — scrape his arm. Michael and the woman run off in different directions, both of them cowering and covering their heads. Michael makes it to a bus shelter and, feeling safer in his plastic blind, looks toward the beach, where the gull is now harrying an elderly man in a bowler hat and Dickensian great-coat. The man is swinging his cane at the bird — awkward parry and thrust — and appears to be smiling, perhaps pleased with the challenge to his otherwise ordinary day.

"Fact: Michael Wiess is the Seymore Langston Watters Distinguished Research Chair in History. After receiving his B.A. from the University of California–Berkeley, he was recipient of the Johns Hopkins University Albert Hardy Fellowship. His academic career began at Arizona State University, where he was Professor of History and Humanities and, eventually, Director of the Interdisciplinary Humanities Program. He was awarded the Matthias Invaarksen Distinguished Teaching Award on two separate occasions…"

Andrew calls from the boardwalk. "Jerome can't get here. We're gonna have to cancel the shoot."

Michael nods. "Wiess is a Fellow of the Royal Historical Society of Britain and recipient of numerous grants and awards, including the Wardrop Fund Grant at the University of Oxford, a grant from the Smith Richardson Foundation, the Bane Fund Grant from Cambridge University and a Hoover Presidential Library Fellowship…"

"Pardon?"

"Nothing. Just thinking out loud."

The President is on CNN, declaring a national state of emergency. Most of the highways on the Eastern Seaboard are closed, and all planes east of Chicago and north of Cincinnati are grounded. The army is being deployed to help with rescue and cleanup efforts, and to — in the President's words — "augment localized law-enforcement activities."

The TV is still on, the sound muted, and while the odd partygoer glances at the screen, it is usually to catch the football updates or comment on Anderson Cooper's relative fuckability.

Michael, who rarely drinks, is quite drunk and passing out shots from an ornate bottle of tequila. He is talking loudly, in part to rise above the din, in part because he has reached the point of the evening when the alcohol is so loud he can hardly hear himself think.

"I only asked because I asked myself the same question, because I felt it was an important distinction to make." He is talking to Jerome, explaining his earlier question. "My answer is that I am getting married because I love him more than I ever thought I could love someone — outside of my children — and because the thought spending my life alone, without him, is almost unbearable."

"He loves you very much, Michael," Jerome says.

"I just worry about...you know. The...Andrew is so into everything...he is so...he is just more, you know, *political* than me."

"You make it sound like a dirty word: *political*."

Michael smiles and leans into an awkward, overly long hug. "Maybe it's the tequila talking — in fact, I'm sure it's the tequila talking — but I love you, Jerome St. Jerome."

Jerome grabs the bottle and pulls it away. "Okay, Dr. Wiess, time we had some coffee."

Michael tries to respond — either agree or disagree, even he isn't sure — and thinks of the birds. They'd done their best to disrupt the ceremony. The first one — a trumpeter swan — striking the tempered glass of the Faculty Club atrium just as the hired musicians — cousin Dion on violin and his partner Eric on bass — launched into a languorous, slightly swinging version of Leonard Cohen's "Hallelujah." As the musicians persevered and the Justice of the Peace cleared her throat to regain the audience's attention, a second bird, a juvenile snow petrel, with its distinctive charcoal-coloured back, crashed into the large glass wall that looked out onto the university's native-plant garden.

The wedding party soldiered on as a small quarrel of sparrows — the correct collective noun, as it turns out, just as Andrew insisted — pelted the window in succession, followed smartly by a pileated woodpecker and then, after a tortuous pause, a ragged blue jay that had somehow wandered several hundred miles out of its range. By the time Michael and Andrew were racing to the car — duly married in a truncated ceremony — birds were falling from the sky, running into trees full flight, colliding with buildings and electrical wires and light stands and neon signs. Even inside, the air smelled of feathers and blood.

"Did you enjoy the ceremony, Dr. Wiess?" Someone

is yelling at him, a young man with blond hair and a lazy eye that makes him more beautiful.

Michael yells something back — "I like that shirt; that colour looks good on you!" — and grabs another bottle from the counter, a single-malt whisky with a Gaelic name that would trip up the soberest of men. He is walking around the kitchen now, topping up everyone's drink. He looks into the darkened living room, where a group of young men — most of whom he has never seen before — are listening to serious electronic music and dancing close, their bodies intertwining.

"Fact," he says, to no one in particular. "While Canada geese do mate for life, the 'divorce' rate is estimated to be between seventeen and twenty-one per cent; extramarital affairs are common."

"You know so many things, Dr. Wiess." It is the boy with the lazy eye. "You have forgotten more than I will ever know."

Michael shrugs. He has an urge to kiss the boy, but instead pours them both a shot of Bunnahabhain eight-year-old.

He finds Andrew alone in the bedroom. The lights are off, and Andrew is looking out the window. Before the dust storms, from this vista — a 1,200-square-foot condo on the seventeenth floor — they could see the lights on the mountains in the distance. Now, only a swirling mocha darkness.

"Have you been crying?" Michael asks.

Andrew turns to him and smiles, a tissue bunched up in his fist.

"Do you know how much I love you, Michael?"

"Is that a rhetorical question?"

"You are drunk."

"That's entirely possible."

Andrew takes Michael's hand and together they step closer to the window.

"Stop swaying, Michael."

"It's not me; it's the room." Michael leans his head on the glass, to steady himself.

"Jerome wants to paint us," Andrew says.

"I'm not sure what that means. English can be very ambiguous at times."

"It means he wants to paint our portrait. As a wedding gift."

Still Life with Fruits, Michael means to say, but is not sure if the words actually come out of his mouth. "I have to lie down, Andrew. I must to bed."

"Just stay with me for a few more moments. It's very peaceful in its way. It's almost beautiful."

Frozen dust is piling on their balcony, drifting nine or ten inches in some spots.

"I used to love standing here, watching the stars."

"Fact: there are one hundred thousand million stars in the Milky Way, and a hundred thousand million galaxies in our universe."

"Really, Michael? Are there really that many? Have you counted them?"

Michael looks into the darkness, trying to see the street lights below.

"Are you mad at me?" Michael asks and, not waiting for an answer, puts both arms around his husband, sliding his hands under Andrew's dress shirt to feel the warmth of his skin, and resting his chin on Andrew's head. There they stand, enjoying the sound of the wind as it ebbs and flows, drawing them into a shared calm that Michael, were he slightly more sober, might describe as bliss. And together they silently count — one, two, three, four and on and on — the birds as they hit the window.

The ladies had agreed: it was a lovely service, even if the minister did go on.

"There was a bit too much of the holy-roller business, I'd say. That really wasn't Elizabeth's cup of tea…" Gillian had worn the yellow pantsuit and the peacock scarf. She liked to dress in bright clothes even when the weather wasn't so bright — as a matter of fact, *especially* when the weather wasn't so bright. That was one of the things the girls liked about her: she knew how to dress bright on drab days.

It was their first Dutch Lunch since Elizabeth passed. The girls had had the waitress set a place for her at the table. It was a tradition they had, the Dutch Lunchers.

The Idea of Ian

"How long has that been going on?" Someone was asking Mrs. Roper about the empty-chair tradition.

"What's that now?" Mrs. Roper may have been pushing a hundred, but she was still smart as a whip.

"She's asking about setting an empty place to honour someone who's passed, Mrs. Roper," Gillian said, holding Mrs. Roper's hand as she spoke. "How long has that been going on?"

Mrs. Roper was cutting through a slice of angel food cake with the side of her fork. "They were doing it before I joined the group and they'll be doing it long after I'm gone." She smiled and put a small piece of cake in her mouth, chewing it with loud, slow smacks.

The waitress came by to top up the coffees. Someone

asked her name and she said it was something like Zari
or Zaria. She had black eyes and raven hair. She looked
very exotic and beautiful in her way. Someone — it might
have been Analee Frost — asked Zari or Zaria if she was
new to the Cosmopolitan, and she told the girls she had
just started working there that week. She was a nice
young woman, and had a baby daughter and lived with
her mother in a small apartment in the Pearl District.
Gillian asked her if she was Italian, and Zari or Zaria
laughed and shook her head.

"I am from Iraq," she said, smiling. "You know, like
the terrorists."

The ladies laughed, and after Zari or Zaria left their
table one of the women — it was Larraine Gautier —
commented on how nice she seemed and how nice her
smile was.

"It's interesting to meet people from other cultures,"
Larraine said. The other girls nodded.

"Ian and I are planning a trip to the Middle East."
Gillian was sipping the last of her Rainier Light and set
the glass on the table as she spoke. She always had a
Rainier Light at Dutch Lunch. She always did the same
thing. She'd hem and haw when the waitress came by
and took their drink orders, and she would ask a bunch
of questions about different drinks and the specials of
the day. Then she'd order a Rainier Light, just like clock-
work. The girls laughed about it, and Gillian didn't mind.
It was one of her quirks, and your quirks make you who
you are as much as anything else.

"The Middle East, my goodness, you are quite the
adventurer." Analee Frost hadn't travelled much since
Earl died, but she was interested in travel and liked to

talk about the travel shows she watched on the Nature Channel. "What countries will you visit?"

"Ian's been there before; he used to do business with a sheik. So he's set everything up. The grand tour: seven cities in twelve days: Dubai, Abu Dhabi, Jerusalem, Cairo, Damascus, Kuwait City, Beirut. We'll see everything."

"I've seen a show on Dubai; it's apparently quite lovely. Arabia, right?"

Gillian made a face. "They call it the United Arab Emirates now, dear."

Analee looked mildly surprised, and then slightly put out. They were always changing the names of things, sometimes, it seemed, for no good reason.

The ladies sat quietly for a moment, sipping their drinks, and then Mrs. Gautier said something or other to Gillian that she, Gillian, couldn't quite understand.

"I beg your pardon, Larraine?"

"I asked if you are going to go see the pyramids."

"Well, yes, in fact we are going to Cairo and are taking a day trip to ride a camel and see the Great Pyramid of Giza."

Mrs. Gautier nodded. "They are supposed to be beautiful. So old. Ancient, really. One of the Seven Wonders of the World."

The other ladies murmured their agreement, and someone — it might have been Mrs. Roper — said it was amazing what people could do when they set their minds to it. They were quiet again, stirring their coffees, relaxing in the quiet comfort of the restaurant.

"I don't think I'd want to ride a camel," Analee said suddenly. "I'll stick to a car, thank you very much." She laughed and looked at the other ladies until, one by one, they began to laugh as well.

One of the ladies repeated the line — *I'll stick to a car, thank you very much* — and they all laughed a little more, and then another one of the ladies said it was too bad Elizabeth wasn't around because she would have enjoyed hearing about the camel ride and Dubai and everything, and would have had a laugh too. If there was one thing Elizabeth loved, it was a good laugh.

The ladies fell silent, sipping their coffees and looking out the window at the autumn rain. Gillian tried to think about Elizabeth because it seemed like the proper thing to do at the moment. And although she and Elizabeth had been close friends — well, as close as you could be with a person like Elizabeth, who was always, frankly, a little standoffish — her mind kept wandering. She hadn't heard from Ian for almost three days, and that was okay. She liked the distance. It was a long-distance relationship, after all; distance was the point.

She'd checked christianseniorssinglemingle.com just before she'd left for Dutch Lunch. There had been one message in her in-box, from a certain Mr. Randall Foster, a pastor from Charlotte, North Carolina. He'd sent a nice message complimenting her on her photo and profile. "You sound like an interesting and accomplished lady," Mr. Foster wrote. "Perhaps we can strike up a correspondence?" Gillian appreciated the nice attention, but — and this was perhaps shallow of her, but's it's the way she felt — she didn't find his profile or picture very appealing. He was wearing a drab tweed jacket and matching (!) tie, sitting in large armchair, bending over a birthday cake with a thousand candles on it. He looked dull and old and, frankly, more in need of a nursemaid than a play-mate or lover. His profile only mentioned that he was a widower and retired minister, searching "for a Christian lady for correspondence" — there was that word again — "and companionship." She always hated when they said that in their profiles: "companionship." It made them sound like they'd given up. Like they didn't want to live anymore, or like they couldn't stand themselves enough to be alone with themselves. If you need a com-panion, get a dog; that was Gillian's opinion, anyways. Still, she sent a nice message back, thanking him for his kind words and wishing him the best of luck in his search for a co-correspondent.

To be honest, she was a little...something. Three days wasn't that unusual, but still, she felt — what was the word? Not quite disappointed. Not quite concerned. Just curious and maybe a tiny bit insecure. They hadn't really seen each other for months, since the trip to Orlando, but that was neither here nor there. And he had told her he was going away to visit his sister in Baton Rouge. He said he might be incommunicado — that was his word — for a few days. His sister didn't have a computer or the Internet. She was a bit of a fuddy-duddy; that's what Ian called her: a "fuddy-duddy"! Of course, she wasn't about to send him a message herself. It was a woman's prerogative to be demure and mysterious. Men liked that; at least, men like Ian did.

Gillian undid her scarf and hung it on the back of her chair. It was a wonderful accessory, fine Mysore silk, gold and blood-red borders, with an intricate peacock-feather design hand-stitched in the centre. Nolan, her first hus-band — her "training spouse," she liked to tell the girls

— had bought it for her on a "business trip" to India shortly after they were married (she always put the phrase "business trip" in air quotes when she was talking about Nolan, since, as she never tired of telling the girls, the only business he did on these trips was monkey business). She'd selected the scarf specifically in honour of Elizabeth; her friend had often commented on how lovely it was and how it always seemed to brighten the room. And if anyone liked someone to brighten a room, it was Elizabeth.

When the bill came, the girls went through the ritual of arguing over who was going to pay for it. It was predictable and amusing and sweet in its own way. Gillian always let one of the other women (it was usually Mrs. Lazlo, whose husband, Neal, had been an ophthalmologist and done very well for himself) pick the check-up. Mrs. Lazlo would make a show of trying to be subtle, picking up the check, then waving her credit card — subtle but obvious — trying to catch the waitress's eye. The other girls would always complain, not wanting to leave Meredith with the whole bill. There would always be a little back and forth, and eventually the bill would wind up in Analee Frost's hands, and she would sit back with her little calculator and figure out exactly how much everyone owed. For her part, Gillian kept her big mouth shut. She didn't mind who paid for lunch, and if it made Mrs. Lazlo feel good to pick up the tab, who was she to deprive her of the pleasure? Lord knows she could afford it. But the paying-for-lunch ritual was part of the ritual of Dutch Lunch itself; it wouldn't have been Dutch Lunch without it.

Gillian found herself giving Larraine Gautier a ride

home from the Cosmopolitan. She's not sure how it happened, but there you are. Don't get her wrong; she *liked* Larraine, it was just that Larraine wasn't her favourite of the Dutch Lunchers. Larraine was a bit of a complainer, and always had something negative to say about someone or something. Today, she was on about the waitress, whom she found to be slow and inattentive.

"I waited I don't know how long for my Reuben sandwich, and when I got it, it was cold. It was like cold rubber."

Gillian wanted to ask Larraine how she knew what cold rubber tasted like — imagine if she'd actually said that! — but kept her mouth shut.

"The Cosmopolitan has gone downhill since Deanna left, if you ask me. Deanna leaving was the worst thing to happen to that place in years."

Again, Gillian held her tongue. She could of pointed out that Annie hadn't worked there for ten years or more, but that wouldn't have made a difference to someone like Larraine. People like Larraine were always looking for something to complain about.

"How's your — nephew was it, Larraine?"

"Hmmm?"

"You know, the boy. The boy. The one who found her? It must have been very upsetting for him, I can't imagine."

"Oh my, yes — poor Jack! I've been worried sick about him. It makes me sick just to think about him finding her like that. You know, he's very mature for his age, but he's still a boy."

There was a pause, as Larraine struggled to squeeze a Scotch mint out of the package. Then: "Grandson."

"Beg your pardon?"

"He's my grandson. Ray's son." Larraine was sucking on the mint as she spoke; it almost drove Gillian crazy.

"Ah, I see."

Another pause, then: "When I was a girl, death wasn't such a big deal. We didn't hide children from it like we do nowadays. It was such a mystery. You lived with it. People died at home, not in some hospital or hospice. I hate the idea of that: hospice. Going away someplace to die. That's what rats do when you poison them. They go away someplace to die. People should die at home."

"Elizabeth died at home, dear."

"Hmmm?"

"Elizabeth died at home; she didn't go anywhere to die. She just died. In a chair, I think. Very peaceful and comfortable."

"Well. You know what I mean."

"I'm afraid I don't know, dear. I think you're saying that things used to be better somehow, that when we were girls, death was somehow better. I'm not disagreeing with you; I'm just saying that death was the same, at least when I was a growing up. Death was something to be avoided at all costs; still is."

Gillian looked at Larraine and smiled a big smile, to show her she was being playful. And at that moment, the car ahead of her must have stopped short or something, and even though she looked back and slammed on the brakes right away, she slid on the wet pavement into the other car.

It was just a little fender-bender really. But somebody called the police and then Larraine had one of her scenes where it was either her back or her heart that was giving out, or maybe both at the same time, and Gillian had to sit there waiting until the ambulance came. It was all a little embarrassing but unnecessary. But what are you going to do? When life hands you lemons, sometimes you just get to sit there and make lemonade.

Of course, she felt obligated to go to the hospital. She really didn't think that Larraine was seriously hurt — it was just a little fender bender — but she was driving at the time of the accident and it would have looked bad if she didn't go to the hospital. She just sat there waiting and waiting in the waiting room till Larraine's son came. He was a very nice man, and talked to her for quite a while about, of all things, gardening. Seems like he was a big gardener, an activity that didn't interest Gillian in its own right, but it sure seemed to interest Roy or Ray — Larraine's son — and he talked and talked and talked about it, even though Gillian was getting a little tired and wanted to go home. Finally, Roy or Ray nodded off and Gillian was able to make her escape — that's how she put it in her mind: she was making her escape. It was cruel in a way, but the truth and kind of funny.

By the time Gillian got home, she was exhausted. She thought of making some tea, but decided she needed something stronger. She got a couple Rainier Lights from the fridge and turned on the computer. She sat at the computer desk in the living room and opened the beer — and only then did she realize that her hand was still shaking. It was strange, because she didn't feel frightened or nervous or angry. She was a little put out, yes — all the unnecessary drama with the ambulance and the police, who now wanted her to get a medical checkup for her driver's licence — and a little embarrassed, but these things happen. People get in fender benders all the time.

She took a deep breath to calm her unsteady hand, then took a long sip of beer.

There was another message from the lonely pastor, Mr. Randall Foster. He asked her a couple of questions — was she a widower, he wanted to know. Did she have children? Did her travels ever take her to the vicinity of Charlotte, North Carolina? She considered his questions for a moment, but felt under no obligation to answer them. She hadn't initiated the conversation with him, and responding again would just send the wrong message. She didn't want to encourage him, and deleted the message.

There was a message from another gentleman, this time from Seattle. His name was Bill White, and his message simply read: "Hey Sexy!" It was accompanied by a picture of Bill on water skis, being towed behind a boat, smiling broadly and giving a thumbs-up to the camera. Gillian was a little put off by the "Hey Sexy" comment, but a little flattered at the same time. She did consider herself sexy for a woman her age and appreciated the attention. She thought about sending a reply to Bill, but changed her mind and almost deleted the message. Seattle was too damn close, in her opinion. What she didn't need right now was a man practically breathing down her neck all the time. Finally, though, she sent him a short reply: "Hello yourself." And that was it.

Gillian finished the end of her beer, and popped open the second Rainier Light. She thought again of sending an email message to Ian, but once again decided against it. A woman's prerogative — that's what she told herself. It was a woman's prerogative to be mysterious and aloof. Ian would get back to her. He always did. That was the beauty of a man like Ian. They liked a little mystery in their lives.

She had one more Rainier Light before she crawled into bed, without bothering to undress. She just wanted to lie there for a moment, alone in the dark, listening to the sound of the rain pelting against the window, and she imagined for a moment that Ian was lying in bed with her. She could almost hear the sound of his breath and feel his body jerking like a dreaming puppy the way it did just before he fell asleep. Was he reaching out for her now, the way he had in Orlando? She imagined herself holding his hand for a moment, caressing his rough fingers, and then, suddenly, letting go of his hand and, ever so gently, pushing him away.

Credits

"Still Life with Birds and Dust" originally appeared in *The Malahat Review*.

"Kaylee" originally appeared in *Event*.

"Dissertation on the Reproductive Habits of Fruit Flies from the Mango Groves of Eastern Uganda" originally appeared in *Sewer Lid*.

ABOUT THE AUTHOR

Christopher Gudgeon is an author, poet and screenwriter.
He's contributed to dozens of periodicals — including
*Playboy, MAD, National Lampoon, The Advocate, Geist,
EVENT* and *The Malahat Review* — and written twenty
books, from critically acclaimed poetry and fiction like
Assdeep in Wonder, Song of Kosovo and *Greetings from the
Vodka Sea,* to celebrated biographies of Stan Rogers and
Milton Acorn, to a range of popular history on subjects as
varied as sex, sexuality, fishing and lotteries. He divides
his time between Los Angeles and Victoria, B.C. Follow
him on Facebook @christophergudgeonbooks and Twitter @1millionmonkies.